RUN TO GROUND

JASPER BARK

Crystal Lake Publishing
www.CrystalLakePub.com

WELCOME
TO ANOTHER

CRYSTAL LAKE PUBLISHING
CREATION

Join today at www.crystallakepub.com & www.patreon.com/CLP

To:

Jim Mcleod, Kit Power and the whole crew at
GingerNuts of Horror,
Tim Cundle and everyone at Mass Movement
Magazine
Michael Wilson, Bob Pastorella, James Everington,
Dan Howarth and the whole This Is Horror massive.

Your continued support has meant the world to me.

HOW DELIGHTFUL TO SEE YOU, GENTLE READER. I TAKE IT YOU'RE HERE FOR ANOTHER SCINTILLATING SLICE OF BARK BITES HORROR? WELL, I PROMISE THIS TERRIBLE TOME WON'T DISAPPOINT.
ALLOW ME TO PRESENT JIM MCLEOD. A MAN WHO'S FEET CAN'T CARRY HIM FAST ENOUGH FROM EVERYTHING THAT MIGHT TIE HIM DOWN AND MAKE HIM GROW UP.
BUT IN THE FOLLOWING TALE HE'LL FACE UP TO MORE THAN HIS RESPONSIBILITIES WHEN HE FINALLY FINDS HIMSELF RUN TO GROUND...

1:

THERE WAS SOMETHING wrong with the shed. Jim knew the moment he saw it.

It was an innocuous little building that sat against the far cemetery wall. Jim kept his tools there, along with his work clothes, the ride-on mower and anything else he needed for groundskeeping.

Yesterday, Cundle had requisitioned it for all his fancy equipment. Jim had moved most of the tools into the bungalow where he lived, on the outskirts of the cemetery. There were a few things he still needed to pick up, and he was curious to see what sort of mess Cundle had made of the place, with all his seismological apparatus.

The first thing Jim noticed, as he drew nearer, was the amount of flies buzzing around the shed. They hovered in a cloud and the noise they made was like a distant engine.

The door was open, creaking on its rusty hinges. There was a thick smell in the air that grew stronger the closer Jim got. It reminded Jim of his father's overalls when he worked at the abattoir.

Jim had no idea what Cundle was doing in the shed but it was time to put a stop to it. He didn't care how high up he was at the university, or how much of an expert he was supposed to be, he was up to no good. Jim wasn't going to let him get away with it, not in his shed.

The cloying smell, and the drone of the flies, increased as Jim reached the door. He put his hand over his nose and mouth as he pulled the door open. A wave of flies swarmed out and Jim waved them away with his free hand.

The dim bulb that hung from the ceiling had been shattered and it took Jim a while to see through the gloom inside the shed. When his eyes had adjusted to the dim light, his brain took a while to process what he was seeing.

Every piece of equipment in the whole shed had been destroyed. The camp table Cundle brought had been knocked aside and bent out of shape. His laptops and seismological apparatus lay in pieces in the corners of the shed.

A stray electric cable, with its torn wires exposed, lay crackling in a pool of water. Except the liquid was too thick to be water, and it was the wrong colour. It was dark crimson and covered the entire floor of the shed. Its surface was beginning to congeal as Jim waded into the shed looking for Cundle. It began to seep into Jim's new trainers.

That's when Jim saw Cundle, and wished he hadn't.

Cundle lay face down with his knees pulled up underneath him. His back was arched. What remained of his head was thrown back and his posterior was in the air. His trousers were torn to shreds and Jim clearly saw the foot-thick column of compacted earth that appeared to have burst up through the boards of the floor and buried itself in Cundle's impossibly distended rectum.

Cundle's buttocks were pushed so far apart to accommodate the shaft of soil, that the flesh around his anus was torn and ruptured. The earth had forced itself so hard and so deep into Cundle's behind it seemed to have pushed every one of his internal organs out the opposite end.

Cundle's mouth had been thrown wide open by the expulsion. His jaw was not only dislocated but the bones had cracked and come apart entirely. The glistening pink tubes of Cundle's lower colon protruded from his torn and ragged lips, spilling out into the lake of blood and bile in front of him. Jim saw what he thought was a liver and a pair of lungs among the coils of dripping innards and the crawling flies.

This couldn't be happening. Jim's mind just couldn't make sense of the scene before him. Who could have done this? How was such a thing possible?

Only this morning Cundle had been fussing around the graves and bossing Jim about as though he was Cundle's lackey. Looking down his nose at Jim the whole time. Now he was reduced to this.

Jim felt a wave of revulsion, then a deep, terrible pity. He hadn't liked Cundle while he was alive. He'd found the man to be pompous and condescending. Jim's menial job left him beneath Cundle's consideration. All the same, he'd been a human being, capable of thought and compassion. He didn't deserve a fate like this.

Jim wondered what Cundle had been thinking in the final moments, as the fear gripped him and the agony of the violation became unbearable? Did he call out for his mother, or his children, if he had any? Did he long for the touch of an old flame, or just pray it would end quickly so the pain would finally stop?

It didn't make any sense. How had the ground just risen up and punched a hole through the floor like that? How had it impaled Cundle and filled him so full of earth that every one of his internal organs had been expelled? Things had been getting weird around the cemetery lately, but this was off the scale.

Jim felt his stomach turn over. Not from the sight of Cundle but from a new smell that invaded the shed. It was growing stronger by the second. He'd thought it was coming from Cundle, but it was too cloying and putrid. It reeked of decay and rotting matter, so rancid it was almost fertile. A shameful sort of fertility, like the mould that grows on dead things. The smell not only grew, it began to envelop him, as though it were alive—another presence in the shed with him.

The floor shook and something beneath the wooden boards rumbled, as though it were moving through the earth directly below the shed. It might even be the thing that had killed Cundle.

Jim's breathing got heavier and his skin went cold all over, even as the sweat broke out on the back of his neck. He realised he was in great danger, not just of death, but the same slow, hideous torture that Cundle would have suffered.

He had to leave the shed right now and put as much distance possible between himself and whatever was under it. Jim turned on his heel and fled into the cemetery.

2:

HE HAD TO get to Sloman's office. Sloman could call the police, or the fire brigade, or whomever it took to fix this. The cemetery was large, covering many acres, but Jim had worked there nearly six months now, so he knew the quickest route.

As he ran down the asphalt path Jim felt the ground beside it rumble. Whatever had been underneath the shed was now chasing him. It was in the earth right beneath him. Something was terribly wrong, things like this shouldn't happen. What had Cundle been doing in the shed to cause this to happen?

Jim's heart pumped and the blood sang in his ears, colours seemed brighter and his vision was sharper. Jim could pick out individual blades of grass and petals on a daisy.

His cousin, a head-case who'd done two tours in Iraq, once told him this happened under fire. In fight or flight situations, all your senses went into overdrive and you knew things without realising how.

Jim was experiencing that now. He couldn't tell how, but he knew whatever was pursuing him wasn't burrowing beneath the earth, it was becoming it. The ground was too smooth and undisturbed for it to be digging. Somehow it was possessing the soil, like a vengeful spirit, converting the earth to whatever it was, then releasing it as it moved alongside the path in pursuit of him.

Jim's pursuer overtook him and circled round in front, becoming the asphalt path in front of him. The asphalt up ahead rippled like it was suddenly gelatinous and the rumbling took on a harsher tone— the growl of a beast about to attack.

Jim turned and ran back up the path, tearing away from whatever was blocking his way. He spotted another path, branching off on his right, it would take him a little off course but he could still circle back and get to Sloman's office. His pursuer followed, keeping time with Jim, sometimes beside the path, sometimes behind him, rumbling loudly like a hound nipping at his heels.

Jim came to a fork in the path and headed right to Sloman's office. Whatever was pursuing him sped up and blocked his way again. Jim was forced to take the other fork. It's playing with me, he thought. Pushing me down the route it wants me to take.

Jim was panting and his lungs were beginning to burn. He wasn't in the best shape and the running was taking its toll. Halfway down the new path he saw the grave. He recognised it instantly. The gravestone was unique; Jim knew every inch of it intimately. The moment he saw it he knew why the thing in the ground had guided him here.

The ground in front of the gravestone had sunk into a deep depression, like a grassy pit. What made it look even odder was the way the turf all around it was folded in on itself. As though the grass was a balloon that had been deflated or the stretched and flabby skin of someone who's undergone rapid weight loss. It had looked very different several days ago.

3:

A Week Earlier . . .

CUNDLE RUBBED HIS bald patch, and sighed. He was a short bloke with a neatly trimmed beard and glasses. His belly hung over the front of his jeans, stretching the trendy T-shirt he wore.

"Any idea what's causing it?" said Sloman, who was tall and thin with a long face and a liking for tweed jackets, which made him look older than he was.

"I do have a theory," said Cundle. "But it's still hypothetical and not very conventional I'm afraid."

Sloman and Jim exchanged a look, Cundle had a habit of talking like he was giving a lecture. Cundle stepped forward and patted the hillock that had sprung up on the grave. The ground all around it was perfectly level, but the grave itself had developed a mini hill that was at least five feet high. Its shape was unusually bulbous and reminded Jim of the distended belly of a famine victim.

The hill had been growing slowly, like a bulge in the earth, for the past three months, getting noticeably larger by the week. The grave was one of three affected in this way, all of them growing large swollen mounds. Jim was very well acquainted with each of the graves and had originally brought the matter to Sloman's attention.

Sloman hadn't thought it important at first, but when the mounds began to swell up into little hills he'd gotten in touch with the cemetery's trustees and they'd found some money to get an expert to investigate. That's when Cundle had been called in. He was a professor at a nearby university.

"I think the graves are being affected by the moon," Cundle said. Jim rolled his eyes and Sloman shook his head to quiet him.

"We know that the moon affects the tides," Cundle continued. "But it's my belief that it has a similar effect on the outer layers of the earth's crust. Usually this effect takes place over such a long period of time we can hardly account for it, but occasionally there are anomalies such as this one. Phenomena that point to the extraordinary effect of the moon on the ground beneath our feet."

"Do you know how we can fix it then?" said Sloman. "Without taking a bulldozer to 'em."

"Oh no, you can't bulldoze these graves. This is a site of great scientific importance. I shall have to come back in a week's time when the moon's at its lowest ebb to do some more tests and then some weeks later when it's at its fullest. All tests will have to be conducted after midnight, so I'll need access to the cemetery then."

Sloman frowned, annoyed that Cundle wanted to study the problem, not fix it. "Jim'll let you in," he said. "He lives on the grounds and he's often up and prowling around at night. Isn't that right, Jim?"

Jim blushed at this. He put his hand in his pocket and adjusted his boxer shorts. A few crumbs of soil fell out and he shook them from his trouser leg without the others noticing.

4:

THE GRAVE HAD fallen in that morning, before Cundle arrived with his fancy equipment. He looked crestfallen when Jim showed him. He had no explanation for the dramatic collapse of the hillock, and didn't understand why it had sunk in on itself in a matter of hours.

Cundle acted as though his precious theory had collapsed along with the grave. He seemed to take comfort in the fact that there had been localised tremors in the area just before the collapse.

As Jim tore past the grave now, he noticed something new. At its foot was a long vertical slit in the earth, almost a gash, where the turf had been pulled apart. In the waning light of the early evening, he could just make out that the gash opened onto a small tunnel.

It took ten minutes to get to Sloman's office from the grave. Jim's legs shook, he knew he couldn't keep up the pace. He wondered for a minute if he shouldn't just lie down on the grave and get it over with. Then he thought of Cundle and what had been done to him and the fear of that spurred him on. Now that Jim had seen the grave, whatever was chasing him seemed content to hover two steps behind him. If he slowed to a walk, it would move closer and worry him, like a sheepdog herding a stray.

Sloman's office was by the main gates, a single storey building with a gabled roof that had once been the cemetery keeper's cottage. Now it served as a visitor's centre and workplace for Sloman. The largest room contained a little display about the history of the cemetery and a few shelves with 'local interest' books. In the back was Sloman's office, a small kitchen and a toilet.

It was usually locked at this hour. Jim fumbled the keys from his pocket as he jogged up. He noticed the main gates were chained and padlocked. Jim hadn't seen the big padlock before and he had no key for it. He had no idea who'd done it, but it changed all his plans. He'd hoped to get the hell out of the cemetery the minute he'd alerted Sloman. Now he'd have to make his way out of one of the side entrances. That meant facing whatever was out there again.

Jim's heart sank the minute he entered the largest room. Something was obviously not right. For a start there was the smell again. It was fainter, but it was definitely there, heavy with rot and a sickening ripeness.

The strip lights in the main room were flickering, but the office out back was in shadow. Jim had expected to hear Sloman at work, typing on his laptop or chatting on the phone. Instead the whole place was dead silent, too silent. The door to the office was slightly ajar. Jim couldn't see beyond it.

He felt like he was in a horror movie. He realised this was the moment when the audience would scream for him to get the hell out, to turn around, run or do anything other than go in that back office. It was one of the reasons he couldn't watch horror movies. He couldn't believe how stupid most of the characters were.

Yet here he was walking towards the office at the back like there was a horrible inevitability to it, as though he had no other choice but to do this. In real life, he thought, sometimes you don't.

Jim pushed open the door and stepped into the office. He let out a sob when he saw Sloman. He sounded like a little school girl. Suddenly he felt very detached from his body, as though he were far away from that office, watching it all from a safe distance.

He hadn't liked Cundle very much, but Sloman was a different matter. Sloman was a decent guy and he'd been good to Jim.

He shook his head and blinked the tears out of his eyes. He couldn't take in what had happened to Sloman, his brain couldn't process it. It was like trying to decipher an unknown language or work out an entirely new branch of mathematics, wholly beyond his comprehension.

Every bit of furniture was shattered. Sloman's laptop, his cable router and his radio lay in tiny pieces on the ground. The walls, floor and ceiling ran with blood and viscera. Thick, viscose droplets fell all about Jim.

The bones from Sloman's disassembled body were scattered around the room in strange geometric arrangements. Bits of cartilage and tendon still stuck to some. Jim couldn't grasp anymore than that, his mind wouldn't let him.

There was a slight tremor in the ground, causing all of Sloman's bones to rattle. The same fetid odour rose in the office like a sudden increase in temperature. Jim started to back out when his foot kicked something that skittered out of the doorway. He turned to look and saw it was Sloman's hand, the only part of his body to remain intact. It had been severed at the wrist but Jim could still see his wedding ring.

The fingers of the hand were clutching something. Jim bent to get a better look and saw it was Sloman's phone. A tiny flutter of hope awoke in him. There might just be a way out of this, he could still call for help. Jim had not owned a phone, a laptop or a tablet since he came to the cemetery. It was one of the things he did to stay off the grid and avoid detection. He regretted that now. He desperately needed to connect to the outside world.

Jim pried the phone from the still warm fingers of the hand and tapped the screen to check for a signal. No bars were showing, but the screen was open on a text conversation. He swallowed hard. He was sure he recognised the number and it made him nauseous. The most recent message had been sent a few hours ago, while Jim had been out weeding. It read:

TY Phil, once again u r a STAR!!! I'll b there soon 2 pick up the spare keys. Don't tell J I'm w8ing for him @ the bungalow. Don't want him 2 do another runner!!! xxx

Jim's hands were so sweaty his fingers were almost too moist to scroll to the top of the conversation. The first message in the conversation, from a week ago, confirmed his worst fears:

Hi Phil, sorry 2 bother u with a txt, but u've been so gr8 and I've been out of my mind since Jim took off. He got rid of his phone and everything. I have so many bills 2 pay and I'm due in just over a month. u don't no wot it means to finally find him. thnx Fi xxx

Jim thought Sloman had been a bit off with him for the past week and now he knew why. Fiona had tracked him down, but how? How had she known he was at the cemetery? Had she guessed why he really came to work here? She'd be the only one who could.

There was another tremor and Jim turned to look back into the office. For the first time he saw the huge hole in the corner. It had been behind him when he entered, so he hadn't seen it. The small pile of soil poking up through the hole began to shake and grow, sending loose earth onto the blood soaked floorboards.

The cloying smell wafted out of the office and Jim knew he had to get to the bungalow. He wasn't certain what he dreaded more, finding Fiona alive or dead.

5:

Six months earlier . . .

JIM ADDED KINDLING to the newspaper and reached for the logs he'd found round the side of the bungalow. It was his first night staying at the cemetery, and he wanted to take the late February chill off the place.

Once he'd built the fire and put a match to it he took the letter from Fiona out of his backpack. He scanned the handwritten pages, working himself up to the task at hand, picking out the key phrases, the ones that enraged him the most:

"This is your baby I'm carrying . . ."

" . . . I want you to stop acting like a child for once and be a man. You can't keep running away from me forever . . ."

"You can't expect me to do this by myself. I need your support and so does your unborn child.

RUN TO GROUND

Even the bright red ink she'd chosen seemed to shake with rage and accusation. She always knew how to push Jim's buttons.

Jim's feelings were hot embers beneath ash. Fiona wouldn't let them just smoulder. She'd blow and blow on the ash until his smouldering resentment burst into flames. Was it any wonder he didn't want to be with her? He fed the pages one at a time into the fire before the anger got too great to control.

It was time to start a new life, kill off his old self and become someone new. Jim McLeod must die, so that Jim McCann could live free of controlling women.

He felt a hollow sadness as the last of the pages curled up and crumbled into ash. Fiona hadn't always been like this. When they first met, she was probably the wildest woman he'd ever come across. He smirked at the phrase 'come across.' It was appropriate though.

She had a hell of a sexual appetite and was more adventurous than any woman he'd ever known. She'd picked him up in some after hours dive that no decent woman would ever frequent. Jim didn't mind, he wasn't looking for a decent woman.

She took him back to her place, trussed him up and broke out the strap on. He'd lain face down on the bed with his ankles tied to his wrists and his butt in the air, wondering just how she'd talked him into it. It didn't stop there though. She wasn't just into filthy acts, she liked to do them in the worst possible places.

Graveyards and cemeteries were her big thing, the creepier the better. There wasn't anything she didn't want to try draped over a tombstone or tied up in a mausoleum. Jim didn't quite know what he'd gotten himself into, but he was hooked. It was a wild and scary ride and he was discovering all kinds of things about himself, finding tastes and predilections he had no idea he had.

For all her wildness, Fiona could still get rather tiring. She was as demanding a girlfriend as she was a lover and Jim liked a quiet life. He was also developing sexual tastes that not even Fiona could satisfy. She may even have guessed this. A certain distance crept into their sex at the end. This might have been because she knew she was pregnant however, and was waiting for the right time to spring her trap.

Jim didn't like it one bit when she did. He'd faced this problem before, but not with someone like Fiona. The minute she found out she was bearing his child it was like she had a chain round his neck.

The kid itself was an even bigger nightmare for Jim. The last thing he wanted was to look after a squalling brat. He didn't want to see it puke and shit its nappy. A man had needs and there was nothing worse than having to put them aside to look after a little tyrant who would scream the house down if he didn't.

There'd be no more attention from Fiona, either. He'd be in constant competition for her affection and he knew who'd win that fight. Women forget about their men when they drop a rug rat. It's like a little switch goes off in their brain and they lose sight of the things that really matter. All they care about is the little parasite in the cot.

So Jim had taken off, like any sensible man would.

He left the city and returned to the tiny little town of St Leonard's. Then he went off the grid so he couldn't be found.

Ironically, he'd left St Leonard's, many years ago, for this self same reason—to avoid being a father. He was really young at the time, an off-comer to the town. Dawn was his first serious relationship and the first woman he ever lived with.

They'd been really happy for about six months, then Dawn showed him her pregnancy tester. She came right out of the toilet with it when he got home from work. Little drops of urine fell from the plastic stick onto the carpet. She was so shocked she hadn't even washed it. They looked into each other's eyes and saw the same fear there.

Jim was too young to cope with that level of responsibility. It brought back all kinds of bad memories from his own childhood. He didn't want to see a repeat of that. He knew there was no way he could hang around and make a go of this. He suggested she have an abortion, said he'd pay for it and everything, but Dawn told him she wasn't brought up to do that sort of thing. She wouldn't hear of it after that. As far as Jim was concerned, that left him no other option.

Maybe he was a coward and maybe he didn't want to see the look of heartbreak on Dawn's face when she found out he wasn't going to be there, but he slipped away late at night without telling her or leaving a note. He packed everything he wanted to keep into the back of his old van and drove away.

Jim didn't give much thought to how Dawn would cope with a child by herself. He didn't think it would be that difficult for her, what with all the state benefits she'd get. He did know that a baby would mean the death of their relationship. He didn't want to hang around and watch it slip away like some ancient relative on life support. He preferred a swift, clean break with less emotional consequences.

It was easier to disappear back then, phones were less complex, not everyone had broadband and there was no social media. Jim did stay in touch with a couple of friends from St Leonard's, those who knew how to keep quiet. That's how he learned what had happened to Dawn.

She had found it too difficult to cope with the burden of bringing up a child by herself. Her father was the only living relative she could turn to. A strict, moral man who terrified her. She was so frightened of what he'd think, having an unmarried mother in the family, that she took an overdose of sleeping tablets.

Jim felt bad then. He didn't know why she'd want to go and do something silly like that. She didn't have to kill herself, she could just have gotten rid of the baby like he'd wanted. He blamed her father in the end for driving Dawn to it.

He didn't think Fiona would try anything that stupid. She just wanted to nail his balls to the floor for getting her pregnant. She couldn't control him sexually anymore, so she was going to use a kid instead. He wasn't going to let that happen. He didn't want to give her the satisfaction.

He knew people would say he was pulling the same cheap trick as before, and this bothered him more than leaving Fiona. Jim cared a lot about what people thought of him, you couldn't fault him there. It was just that he also knew the things he could and couldn't do, such as being a parent. You couldn't blame him for knowing his limitations.

Fiona should have known better than to hound him until he left. She'd be really pissed off when she couldn't find him, and if she ever did, she'd tear his balls off. Jim planned to stay away from women for a while, it was a lot safer. Besides, the way his sexuality was heading, he probably wouldn't need them.

6:

HALFWAY TO THE bungalow Jim's lungs were burning and his legs shook. He stopped and bent forward with his hands on his knees, trying to catch his breath. He was more out of shape than he realised. Coming up behind him he heard the familiar rumble on either side of the path. There seemed to be two of them now. There was twice as much noise and the ground on either side of the path shook.

They rumbled ominously at his heels and he stumbled into a brisk trot. "Alright, alright," Jim said. "I'm going." Despite his fatigue and his mock bravado Jim was very, very afraid. He'd seen what those things could do and he knew they were playing with him.

He came to a crossroads in the path and his pursuers cut in front of him blocking two of the paths, including the most direct route to his bungalow. He knew where they were taking him. He gasped for breath and his head throbbed as he jogged past the second of the three affected graves. Like the first, the huge hillock had caved in and was now a pit filled with folds of loose turf. At the foot of the grave there was another slit in the ground that also led onto a small tunnel. Once again the turf had been folded back on either side of the slit and Jim was struck by the similarity to a pair of female labia.

He stopped dead still at this, trying to process his feelings. His two pursuers began to circle him from below. As they closed in, his legs shook so much he couldn't tell if it was fear or the ground vibrating. Jim leaped forward and began to run again, drawing on hidden reserves and pure desperation.

He now had no doubts about what he'd find when he got to the bungalow. He placed a hand on the door lintel, struggling to get a grip on himself. He was terrified to enter, but he was even more afraid to stay outside. As he opened the door he felt that cool and sickening feeling in his gut that comes with an awful sense of premonition.

Fiona's scent was the first thing that struck him. He'd know it anywhere, a mixture of patchouli and fresh leather. Hanging under it was the thick coppery odour of blood, and then he was hit by the familiar cloying putrescence that had marked the last two murder scenes.

Fiona, or what remained of her, was in the living room, arranged around a giant pile of earth that had broken through the flagstone floor.

Jim was overwhelmed by what he saw. This was so much worse than what had been done to Sloman and Cundle, there just weren't words to describe it. Jim stood for a moment with his mouth hanging open, his jaw moving up and down as though trying to form words, or simply find a sound to describe how he was feeling.

The ground beneath him swayed. The walls seemed to rush at him then recede just as rapidly. He wondered if the strange creatures in the ground were doing this, but then his legs went from under him and he fell to his knees.

His stomach could no longer hang on to its contents and Jim felt it contract violently as a wave of nausea burst through him. He leaned forward and threw up, sobbing between heaves. He breathed a ragged sigh and choked on his own vomit. This didn't stop him bringing more up and he coughed and cried and puked and then he let go of his bowels in panic.

Jim had been intimate with the flesh that was shredded and scattered over the dirt covered floor. He'd kissed and stroked the skin that lay draped in tatters across the broken furniture.

It wasn't just Fiona in the living room. In amongst her desecrated remains was Jim's unborn child. The enormity of this suddenly hit home and Jim felt an immediate and wrenching sense of loss. He'd spent seven months trying to avoid being a part of this child's life, to sever all ties with its mother, and now that those ties were irrevocably cut, he felt nothing but regret. Deep aching regret.

Jim might not be long for this world. Now nothing of him would survive it. He didn't know what the things in the ground had planned for him, but he knew it wasn't going to be pleasant. This child might have been the one thing he could have left to the world and they'd taken that away from him. Torn its tiny, frail form apart before it even had a chance to breathe.

The terror and loss that sat like a hard lump on Jim's chest turned to anger. "Fuck you," he shouted as he got to his feet. "Fuck you, whatever the fuck you are. You do not get to do this. You are not going to beat me!" He wiped the vomit from his chin and adjusted the front of his jeans which were uncomfortably wet.

The same putrid smell wafted into the room, its strength intensifying as if in reply. "Fuck you," he said again, and kicked at the pile of earth. Jim stomped from the living room and left the bungalow.

There was a small side entrance no more than a hundred yards from Jim's bungalow. It was his best way out of the cemetery. He didn't know if the single wrought iron gate would be padlocked, too. If it was, he would just clamber over the wall.

Could his underground tormentors follow him out of the cemetery? He hoped not. It was a short walk to the centre of town. He could get help. Why hadn't he tried to look for Fiona's phone, or kept hold of Sloman's? It was too late for that now. He'd just have to depend on his speed and cunning.

Jim took off at a sprint, drawing on reserves of energy he didn't know he had. As he approached the side entrance, which wasn't padlocked, his two pursuers tore along the side of the path and overtook him. Jim picked up speed, pushing himself beyond his limits.

As he got within a few feet of the gate, the ground on either side of the path before him started to crack. The fissures in the soil grew rapidly until there were two sinkholes. Jim slowed his pace, wary of what might happen next.

Without warning a fierce spray of soil issued from both of the holes, like two brown fountains sending up jets of fine earth. The soil fell on the path in front of the gate and within seconds a great mountain of dirt had formed, blocking Jim's way to the gate. There was no way he could get around the heap of dirt without going off the path, and that's where his pursuers lurked. He thought about trying to climb it, but it was at least nine feet high and made entirely of loose earth. Earth was their element. There might be worse things hiding in the pile than lurked at the sides of the path.

Jim cast about for another course of action. There must be some way out of this, somewhere he could go to evade these things. Then he remembered the church, St Dunstan's, on the other side of the cemetery. If he could get there, he could claim sanctuary from whatever was chasing him. The church was a holy place, a refuge from dark forces, surely he'd be safe there? Jim wasn't the most religious person, but he knew that whatever was chasing him wasn't natural, and under those circumstances you needed something pretty big like God on your side.

Jim set off at a jog, panting hard and trying to ignore the cramp in his leg and the stitch in his side. A third underground tormentor had joined the other two. He could feel it switch from one side of the path to the other, occasionally rumbling up behind him with menace.

Jim didn't bother to take the most direct route to the church. He knew where his pursuers wanted him to go. The third grave was only a few minutes from the church, and he headed straight for it. Like the other two graves it had a distinctive headstone with an angel on it, one that Jim knew well. The hillock that had once grown out of it had also collapsed and at its foot Jim saw another gash in the earth with the turf folded back like a pair of labia. The little tunnel behind them looked for all the world like a birth canal.

Jim turned a bend and St Dunstan's loomed up ahead of him. It was an imposing church, almost the size of an Abbey. It looked far too grand for a tiny rural town like St Leonard's. The rear wing of the church was the original, medieval building. The rest of the building was an eclectic mix of Corinthian columns, battlemented parapets and Gothic stone reliefs featuring gargoyles and saints.

Jim thought of the vicar, Father Powers. He would know what to do. He was the one person in St Leonard's that Jim trusted most. He just prayed the old man was alive and unharmed.

7:

Two Months Earlier . . .

JIM WAS JUST putting the weed puller back in his tool shed when he saw the snow-white hair of Father Powers moving between the gravestones. Jim wiped the sweat from his brow as the elderly vicar stepped into view. He was a short man with a ruddy complexion and wild grey eyebrows that sat atop bright brown eyes. He was thickset, with powerful broad shoulders and big rough hands that suited a builder or a boxer better than a man of God.

"Now then, Jim," he said with a smile. "Why such gloomy features on a beautiful day like this?"

"Was I gloomy, Father Powers? I didn't realise."

"'Was I gloomy?' he says, with a face like thunder. And I've told you before, lad, it's Kit. I'm not with my parishioners now, there's no need to stand on ceremony."

"Sorry, Father Pow . . . I mean Kit, I've never been on first name terms with a vicar before. I keep forgetting."

"I'll wager you've not been on any kind of terms with a vicar before, eh, lad?"

"No," said Jim, and they both chuckled. "I didn't

realise I looked down, I've just been brooding a bit I guess."

"You're being pursued by demons of your own making, lad, that's what it is. You need to unburden yourself, you'll feel a lot better for it."

"Wait, are you telling me confession is good for the soul? Isn't that what the other lot say?"

"The papists you mean? You think we Anglicans are all about repression and keeping it bottled up? No, lad, I've heard as many confessions as the unmarried men in frocks, I can tell you."

Jim smiled at Father Powers' depiction of Catholic priests. The old man held up a tartan thermos. "Will you join me for a coffee? It has a little something extra in it, if you catch my drift." Father Powers was fond of his brandy. Jim nodded and followed the old man to the nearest bench.

He liked the vicar a lot. It was Father Powers who got him the job tending the grounds. Jim had spent a lot of time in the cemetery during his first few days back in St Leonard's. He'd needed time to himself, to figure things out and contemplate his new urges.

Father Powers had seen Jim hanging around and came over to chat one day. He asked if Jim had recently lost a loved one. Jim explained that he just liked the cemetery, it gave him the solitude he needed.

The vicar had a way of drawing people out of themselves and getting them to open up. He soon learned that Jim was newly back in town and in need of money. He told Jim the cemetery was looking for a groundskeeper and he'd put in a good word with the trustees. Two days later Jim went for an interview and was offered the job on the spot. The pay was lousy, but it came with a one-bedroom bungalow so he didn't have to worry about meeting his rent.

Since then, Jim had gotten quite close to Father Powers. He didn't attend any of his church services, only about five people in the whole town did, but he ran into the old man at least every other day and they always made time to chat.

Jim sipped the sweet black coffee laced with brandy. The cup had an old plastic smell that reminded him of drinking tea from his grandma's thermos on picnics by the sea. "I see you had some workmen in again yesterday," he said.

"Yes, we're getting some work done on the nave. Plus, we need to reinforce the buttress at the south end. It's going to cost a pretty penny."

"I imagine these old places need a lot of repair and upkeep."

"And you're probably wondering how such a tiny parish can subsidise all this work? Am I right, lad? I mean it's not like the collection plate is overflowing come Sunday."

"I didn't want say anything, but I've always wondered how such a tiny little town came to have a church that was so big and . . . and . . . "

"Ornate?"

"Well . . . yeah. I mean I'm not trying to be funny or anything. I'm just, y'know, curious."

"That's quite alright, you're not the first to have wondered about this. I like you, Jim, so I'll let you in on a little secret. Did you know there's a whole network of tunnels running under St Leonard's?"

"No, is that like a war effort thing or something?"

"No, these tunnels are much older than any war effort, millennia older."

"So who built them?"

"Most of them are naturally occurring, some were excavated, but not by human hands, or not by anything we would recognise as human these days. Some of the tunnels go down miles beneath the earth."

"Does . . . does anyone know about this?"

"The locals have known about it for centuries. The real locals that is, not the off-comers from the city who've been buying up all our houses recently. No offence meant, lad."

"That's okay, none taken."

"A couple of hundred years ago, when the town was just a farming community, hardly changed since the medieval days, a young vicar came to town, my predecessor. He was something of a naturalist and an amateur archaeologist, as were many churchmen in Victorian times. When he heard the rumours about the tunnels, from his parishioners, he set out to learn more. It was believed that a great treasure lay somewhere in the tunnels, deep underground. You can imagine what effect this had on the imagination of an intrepid young priest, keen to make his name in the world of letters. He was warned that a hideous monster, a Byrfling the locals called it, prowled the tunnels, to keep away the unwary and guard the treasure."

"I take it that didn't stop him."

"Indeed it didn't. After a lot of local exploration, he found an entrance to the tunnel hidden in a mausoleum in the grounds of St Dunstan's."

"Is the mausoleum still there, will I have seen it?"

"No, it was pulled down many years ago. The land it stood on is beneath the church now."

"So what did he find in the tunnels then? Was there a Byr . . . thingy?"

"Byrfling. He wasn't torn apart, if that's what you're asking, but after much exploration and many months spent mapping all the tunnels, he did come across some very curious non-human remains."

"What sort of remains?"

"Skeletal remains, most of which are now in a private collection I believe. When roughly assembled it appeared to be a giant creature that walked on two legs."

"If there was a monster in the tunnels, how come no one's ever heard of this?"

"Well that's partly to do with why the church is so rich."

"There really was treasure down there."

"Not the type of treasure you'd normally associate with underground passages, but my predecessor did find a repository of immense and quite unbelievable value."

"What was it?"

"A vast store of scrolls."

"Scrolls?"

"Written in a language that predates any human tongue, on the tanned hides of animals that have been extinct since the Cretaceous period."

"What? How is that even possible? How could he have known they were that old?"

"There were other scrolls and written material down there, some of it in early human languages that we can read. There was even a key of sorts that allowed a translation of the other scrolls."

"Did he translate them, then?"

"Some of them. It's a difficult business and it wasn't his forte, if I'm honest. There are many scrolls and their translation is a long and painstaking business. It's been the life-work of many of my predecessors and progress is still slow."

"So where are the scrolls now?"

"They're still down there."

"All of them?"

"Most of them, a few were sold off for exorbitant sums to certain collectors, but the majority are kept safely out of view. That's what St Dunstan's and its clergy are paid to do."

"I'm sorry, I don't quite understand."

"There are many rich and powerful figures in the Church who do not want the revelations in the scrolls to ever come to light. The truths they contain are too damaging, not just to their faith, but to every religion currently followed by man. Simply put, what they outline is heresy. A heresy capable of changing the consciousness of everyone on the planet. Since their discovery, my predecessors and I have been paid to guard them. We translate the scrolls as best we can, and we ensure that no one will ever read them."

"No one?"

"Not a soul."

"And they pay you really well?"

"Our current reserves are astronomical. We can't draw attention to ourselves by spending too much of it, but it paid for the church and this cemetery to be built and it continues to finance their upkeep."

"I'm going to have to ask for a raise then."

Father Powers laughed at this and put his hand on Jim's shoulder. "Now, lad, I've confided in you, told you a little secret that could get us both killed if it was to come out. That's how much I trust you. Isn't it time that you showed me the same trust?"

"What do you mean?"

"You know very well, lad. I want you to tell me what's troubling you?"

Jim looked into Father Powers' deep brown eyes and saw the compassion and understanding there. He found he did want to unburden himself.

"I . . . I'm afraid of what you might think of me," he said.

"Don't be afraid of what I might think, lad, it's God you've got to make things right with."

"How do I do that?"

"The first step is to take ownership of your sins and confess."

So Jim took a deep breath and told Father Powers all about Fiona and how he had left her high and dry, then he took an even bigger breath and told the kindly old man about Dawn and how he'd left St Leonard's in the first place to escape his responsibilities as a parent. He couldn't bring himself to tell Father Powers about Dawn's suicide though, he didn't want to completely lose the old man's good opinion.

Father Powers smiled and patted his shoulder. "That's a big thing to admit to, lad, and I'm proud of you for finding the strength. Now why do you think you're so scared of being a father and raising a child?"

Jim didn't have an immediate answer for that. He cast his mind back to when both women had told him they were pregnant and then he went back even further, to when he was fourteen and his mother told him she was pregnant.

RUN TO GROUND

For the whole of his formative years it had just been the two of them. She was a single mother and he was her little prince. She spoiled Jim rotten and he loved it. He was the centre of her world and she couldn't do enough for him.

This hadn't changed when she'd started seeing Duncan. Jim hadn't been happy when his mother got a boyfriend. He was afraid that she wouldn't have time for him anymore, but that couldn't have been further from the truth. In fact, he got more attention, because Duncan took a great interest in him. He took Jim fishing, taught him how to fix up cars and even let him ride a motorbike by himself.

Then his mother dropped her bombshell and everything changed. Jim had a bad feeling about the pregnancy from the minute she told him. The bigger she got the more she neglected Jim. Duncan, on the other hand, was great at involving him. He used to talk to the baby all the time in the womb. One time he called Jim over and told him to speak to his little brother.

"Will he hear me?" Jim said.

"No, of course not, silly," said his mother.

"Yes he will," said Duncan. "They've done scientific tests on this. The baby listens and responds and everything."

"What do I have to do?"

"Just put your mouth up to your mother's tummy and speak to him."

"What shall I say?"

"Anything you want."

What Jim wanted to say was: 'I hope you die inside there, you little bastard.' Instead he just mumbled "hello", then got so self conscious he had to leave the room.

The moment Jim's mother came back from the hospital with the screaming red bundle, every one of Jim's worst fears were realised. Previously his mother had done everything for him, now she couldn't even be bothered to fix him a meal. He was lucky if she remembered to wash his clothes or tidy his room for him.

All his mother's attention was taken up with his newborn brother, a shrieking, piss and shit factory who threw constant tantrums and stopped everyone in their tiny apartment from sleeping more than two hours a night. In spite of this, his mother did nothing but coo and dote on the demanding little creature. She didn't have time for anything else.

If she did pay Jim any attention, it was only to nag him for not doing something or complain about how tired she was and that he wasn't helping her enough with his little brother. Like he'd want to do anything for that evil little thing, other than put a pillow over its face.

Jim wasn't the only one who felt neglected. His mother paid less and less attention to Duncan and didn't realise she was slowly freezing him out.

Jim came home from school one day to find his mother in pieces on the bathroom floor. His little brat of a brother was screaming as usual, but Jim wasn't interested and, for once, neither was his mother. "He's gone, James, oh James, oh my little Jimmy," she sobbed. "Duncan, he's left me."

She reached out her arms to Jim, but he stayed where he was in the doorway. The sight of his mother disgusted him. He felt no pity for her after the way she'd isolated him, and he could understand perfectly why Duncan had left. He was going to miss him like hell, but he admired Duncan for going. It was what his mother deserved and Jim realised that he would have left too if he could.

In that moment, the future of all Jim's relationships was decided. He'd learned that men, real men, don't stand for that sort of neglect. They move on and find someone who's really going to appreciate them, and women put newborn babies before everything else. The minute they have one, they stop loving you like they did before.

At the time, Jim didn't realise he was pissed off at his mother because he missed her, missed how close they'd been. If he could have gotten over his anger he would have seen that he really wanted nothing more than to regain that closeness, to be the centre of her world again.

Late at night, as he lay in bed listening to his mother cry herself to sleep, he'd indulge in a strange fantasy.

It wasn't like the fantasies he had about the popular girls in school. In this fantasy he used to imagine what it would be like to return to his mother's womb, to be inside her once again, part of her body and her sole concern.

He knew it was impossible, but at the time it seemed like the only way he could connect with her again. She'd chosen the baby over him and he could never forgive her. He would never forgive any woman who did that to him.

Jim didn't share any of this with Father Powers.

The two of them sat silently on the bench with their own thoughts. Father Powers finished the last of his coffee and got to his feet.

"Well, Jim," he said. "I've things to be attending to and I'm sure you have, too. You have a lot to think on in the meantime. Don't forget, you can always call on me at the church, if you're ever in need of my help."

8:

GOD SAVE US, Jim, you look a state," said Father Powers as Jim burst into the vestry.

Jim was just glad to see him alive. Father Powers took a step back and wrinkled his nose. Jim glanced down at his T-shirt and jeans. They were stained with blood, soil, and urine. For the first time he noticed that his boxers were sticking to his butt cheeks and there was a hardening lump back there. No wonder he reeked.

"Father . . . Father Pow . . . I mean Kit," he said panting, as much from panic as from the run. "There are things out there . . . in the cemetery. They're under the ground, they come from the graves, the ones Sloman was worried about. They're killing people, Sloman and Cundle and . . . and . . . It's horrible, they've been chasing me."

"I know all about them, lad."

Jim was incredulous. "You do?"

"I heard them coming."

"You did?"

"I can feel them in the ground. They're outside now. They won't come in the church though."

Jim began to cry with relief, like a little child. He

hated for Father Powers to see him like this, but he couldn't stop himself. "Oh, God Father, what they did . . . what they did to them . . . you can't imagine . . . "

"Now, lad, that's enough of that. Come with me, we can't stay here in the vestry."

Jim followed Father Powers to the front of the church. He would have followed him anywhere at that moment in time. He was just grateful to have someone take charge and tell him what to do. Every attempt he'd made to escape his pursuers or outwit them had failed. Finally, he had someone he could rely on, who knew what to do.

Father Powers stopped by a small side entrance at the front of the church. The aged wooden door was studded with cast iron rivets. Father Powers pulled out a set of almost medieval looking keys and put one in the lock. The door swung open with an impressive creak. Beyond were a narrow set of winding stairs.

Father Powers reached up to a little wooden shelf on the inside of the door and took down a large flashlight. "You remember I was telling you about that old entrance to the tunnels?"

"This is it?" said Jim.

Father Powers nodded. "This is it. Now stay close, it's dark down here and we've only the one torch."

The steps were narrow and worn to smooth, polished depressions in the middle. The temperature dropped and became almost freezing as they descended. Jim's arms came up in goose bumps.

"Do you . . . do you know what those things are?" said Jim.

"They're Byrgen," Father Powers told him. "Or Byrgen-Beorden, to give them their full title. It's from the Anglo Saxon, roughly translated it means 'grave-child' or 'born-of-the-grave.'"

"So they were actually born . . . I mean they did come out of those three graves, the ones that were affected?"

"Those are good questions, lad, but aren't you a little curious as to how I know about them at all?"

"Did you read about them in those scrolls you mentioned?"

"Good lad, yes I did. In fact, as I was the one who translated the scrolls, I was the first to read about them in a very long time."

"So you know what they're doing here?"

"First things first, lad. Now, did you ever hear tell of an ancient moon goddess called Monanom?"

"No."

"No, I didn't imagine you would have. She's unusual in that, while most goddesses are individual or tripartite, she's two-fold. She's similar to the Roman god Janus, who had two faces on either side of his head, but she has two whole fronts on either side of her body, and no back. One side of her was a beautiful, chaste young maid, the other was an evil crone. The Maiden was in love with the sun god, but they could never consummate that love because the sun god can never learn of her sister, an evil crone who spends all her time in darkness plotting."

The steps levelled off into a narrow stone walkway. Jim followed Father Powers to the end of it where he produced another key and unlocked an even more ancient door.

"Both sides of Monanom had their followers," Father Powers continued. "The crone attracted women and men who craved power, or revenge on those who've wronged them. She taught them certain malign crafts. Students of the occult talk of the 'left hand path,' the earliest depictions of Monanom always draw her on the left hand side of her sister, hence the origin of the name."

"But what does this have to do with those beer-guns?"

"Byrgen. We'll get to that in a moment. First I want to talk to you about grave eggs."

"Grave eggs?"

The steps on the other side of the ancient door were even narrower, and curved down in a spiral. Jim had to place his palms against the damp, chilly walls to keep from losing his footing.

"Yes, this is one of the most difficult and deadly workings that Monanom taught to her followers," said Father Powers. "It crosses every barrier of the natural order and turns a resting place for the dead into a vessel for unborn life. To create one, you have do some ungodly and unspeakable things, lad. Things no decent, sane human being would ever consider, but that's what it takes to create any object of immense power."

"What do you do with these grave eggs?"

"You plant them in a grave or a place of burial, and they grow."

"Grow?"

"Yes, grow, just as a normal mammalian egg grows inside its mother, drawing on the same matter she's composed of to form a foetus, the grave egg draws on everything a grave is composed of to create a blasphemous mockery of life. All it needs to activate it is the right insemination."

RUN TO GROUND

They reached the bottom of the steps. The ground beneath their feet changed from stone to closely packed earth. Jim felt a cold sickness settle in his gut when Father Powers mentioned 'insemination'. He suddenly felt anything but safe with the old man, whose mood and attitude had changed both subtly and irrevocably.

"This is one of the few parts of the tunnel network that isn't entirely rock," Father Powers said. "Which makes it ideal for our purposes."

Jim suddenly felt a familiar rumbling. It was coming from the soft clay walls now, not the ground. It was faint and distant but gathering momentum, getting closer all the time. They were coming from three directions, possessing the earth around them, twisting it into whatever sickening form they took, then moving on. Leaving the soil spent and violated, even at this depth. Jim was unbelievably far beneath the ground, but he still wasn't safe.

He was halfway down the tunnel when he realised the rumbling was coming from behind him. Shit! Jim stood still and listened. They were cutting off his exit, putting themselves between him and the steps back to the surface. He was going to be trapped down here with them if he didn't do something right now.

In the brief moment that Jim had stood still, Father Powers had disappeared into the gloom of the tunnel ahead, taking the flashlight with him. The tunnel was thrown into darkness.

In blind panic Jim raced forward to catch up with Father Powers, but he couldn't see where he was going. He collided with one of the ancient earthen walls and bounced off it. A sharp pain shot through his temples and his face stung.

He staggered backwards and his feet went from under him. He landed with a wet thud on his back, the breath knocked out of him. The dry, hard soil of the floor was surprisingly cold. He fought to catch his breath and stop his head reeling. The rumbling built to a frenzy behind him.

Then it stopped quite suddenly, and transformed into a thick slithering sound. Like wet cement or earth being poured from a great height. A familiar putrid smell flooded the tunnels, stronger now and more acrid. Jim gagged and felt bile burn the back of his throat.

The things were fully in the tunnel now. Jim could feel they were. He could hear them, but the sounds weren't like anything Jim had heard before. He couldn't begin to imagine what they were doing to make that sort of noise and he honestly didn't want to.

It was at that point that Father Powers chose to turn around and walk back up the tunnel towards Jim. He let the flashlight travel over the three figures, what had he called them? Byrgen, that was it. He chuckled as the beam revealed them, a bitter, mirthless laugh.

Jim couldn't quite recognise what he was seeing, nothing in his life had prepared him for the sight and he had nothing to relate it to. The three Byrgen filled the tunnel, large lumbering forms that had arms and legs but no head and no recognisable human shape.

They seemed to be comprised of soil. There were also roots and gravel and aged bones, plus rotting human flesh in their makeup. At the top of their bodies, where a head or neck ought to have been, was a gaping orifice filled with tier upon tier of sharpened teeth. The teeth were made from shards of shattered coffin wood or mangled brass fittings, as were the long talons on the end of their many fingers.

The talons reached out for Jim. The orifices on the tops of their necks pulsed, opening and closing as they ground their sharp little teeth together. In the centre of what passed for their chests were two huge rheumy pits that could have been eyes or some other sense organ. They leaked pus and seemed to gaze right into Jim with recognition and with a desperate need. It was the same need he'd seen in the eyes of his newborn brother looking at their mother.

Jim pushed himself up and clambered to his feet. He was going to have to run again. He was so close to total exhaustion that his arms and legs were twitching and shaking. These things had chased him round the entire cemetery, and now that he finally saw them, they were worse than anything he could have imagined.

The only reserves of energy he had left lay in his utter desperation. Jim turned away and started to run past Father Powers. The vicar stepped in front of him with his hands up. He pushed Jim in the chest with more strength than Jim thought possible for a man his age.

Jim toppled over and landed on his backside. The last ounce of strength drained from Jim's body and the fight went out of him. He sat there like a discarded rag doll in the jaws of a terrier. The cold of the hard ground crept through his buttocks, down his thighs and up his spine.

"You don't get to run away this time, lad." Father Powers said. "You have to be a man now and face up to your responsibilities. They're your children, lad, and they need you."

Children? My children? Jim's mind was fighting against the possibility, but his gut had already accepted it.

He understood what Father Powers had planted in those graves and why they had swollen with life. Worse yet, Jim knew he was the one who had actually caused this.

9:

Four months ago . . .

THE MOON WAS at its lowest ebb and this was a secluded corner of the cemetery. The night sky was cloudless but it was still very dark. Jim stood for a moment, letting his eyes get used to the gloom. All the better to see the grave, to admire its beauty.

It was the third one he'd chosen and he knew it was going to be the last. He was a loyal person, after all, and he didn't want to spread himself too thinly. It was the headstone that attracted him, it always was. He liked a well kept and perfectly shaped plot, but it was the headstone that really did it for him.

The headstone had to be ornate and quite unique, without too much ageing or wear. He wasn't interested in anything too weathered, or utterly dull. If there was another like it, anywhere in the cemetery, then you could forget it. And it had to have a carved angel on it. Some men liked blonde hair, big butts or long legs, Jim liked angels.

He'd been flirting with the grave for a while, taking any opportunity he could to drop by. He'd mown its grass and weeded its plot, until it was the prettiest little grave in that part of the cemetery.

On their first date he brought a bottle of wine and they just cuddled. When he'd finished the wine and it was time for him to go, Jim couldn't resist leaning forward and placing a long kiss on the alabaster toes of the angel. He hadn't meant to be so forward and he didn't intend to rush things, but he just couldn't resist.

On their second date things had gotten a bit more intimate. Jim had kissed every inch of the headstone, breathing in its mineral scents. Then he'd licked and stroked practically every blade of grass that grew on the grave. His mouth and chin were stained green and brown when he left.

Tonight was the third date. Jim intended to get lucky.

It was Fiona who woke this urge in Jim. Towards the end of their relationship he'd tired of her. The only thing he still found exciting was the graveyard sex. Then he realised it wasn't Fiona that turned him on, it was the graves.

This first hit Jim in the 'out of town cemetery' they liked to break into. It could even have been the night he got her pregnant. He was finding it hard to come. He was rock hard inside Fiona and she was loving it, but Jim couldn't seem to find the vinegar strokes to take him over the edge.

He tried to turn himself on thinking about how disrespectful it was to thrust himself deep into Fiona on top of someone's final resting place. Then he thought about the soft earth of that resting place and the hard gravestone thrusting out of the ground. He started to imagine what it would be like if Fiona wasn't there, if it was just him and the grave and he was penetrating the warm soil instead of her.

RUN TO GROUND

This made Jim come so deep and so hard it was like an out of body experience. The next few times they did it in graveyards, Jim tried to get closer to the grave than to Fiona, and that's when she might have guessed about the impulses growing in him. For Jim, that was the moment the relationship ended. When she told him she was pregnant, it only confirmed his need to leave and never see her again.

Jim knew his new urges couldn't remain a fantasy for long. Sooner or later he was going to act on them. That was his main motivation for taking the job at the cemetery. He would have his pick of eligible graves.

He'd had two so far, and now he intended to take a third. Jim decided to dispense with foreplay, he was already hard from the anticipation. He knelt down and ran his fingers over the grave's turf, fondling and probing until he found the sweet soft spot.

Every grave has that perfect place for penetration, where the soil gives the most. He took out a trowel and cut through the turf, removing a core sample and leaving a hole just large enough for him to enter. A little water from a bottle in his other pocket turned the earth to mud, a perfect lubricant.

Jim pulled down his jeans and freed his erection. Then he eased himself into the hole. Something was wrong though. He wasn't feeling it like he usually did. It wasn't the grave, it was Jim. He'd had a lot on his mind recently and he was starting to wonder what would happen if anyone caught him at this.

He was pretty sure it wasn't illegal, well not much anyway. He'd probably just get off with a fine. What worried him was what other people would think of him if he did get caught. These things were important to Jim.

He wasn't a pervert or a kiddy fiddler. He wasn't hurting anyone with his passion. But he still didn't know how he'd justify what he was doing if anyone did find out. He knew that very few people would understand, unless he made them, and he didn't have the words for that.

A grave was the perfect lover because it could never conceive. It was a vessel for the dead, not the living. It represented death in all its forms because it was where all the living end up. When Jim had his cock in a grave he was fucking death itself, denying it had any power over him. It was the ultimate affirmation of life.

This thought stirred Jim and he began to thrust harder into the grave. The French call orgasms 'the tiny death'. He didn't know why, but he was struck with the certainty that this tiny death would break the hold any larger death had over him.

For some reason, as he came, he was reminded of the fantasy he used to have about being back inside his mother's womb. He would beat death and return to the womb and no baby would ever steal a woman from him again.

Jim lay panting on the cool earth. He was spent and flushed with a happy afterglow. His satisfied high was short lived. As he lay pressed to the grass, listening to the steady rhythm of his heart, he heard something in the ground beneath him. It was the faintest of rumbles, but it caused his balls and his cock to shrivel up inside him with a sudden chill.

It felt, for the briefest moment, like something had opened up within the ground to catch what he'd left there. The thought of this terrified Jim, as though it was the worst thing that could be done to him.

10:

FOR A LONG time, Jim tried to deny the enormity of what the Byrgen had done to him. He felt certain they were going to kill him when they fell on him in the tunnel. After they were done, Jim almost wished they had.

As they'd advanced on him, Jim saw they were carrying trophies from their other kills. They had the skins of all three victims, at least one of which they must have collected after Jim found the remains. He also saw Fiona's umbilical cord and some of Cundle's organs.

Jim looked to Father Powers in silent appeal but the old man's face was grim and implacable. "It's no use trying to get out of it now, lad," he'd said. "The Bible tells us, 'As ye sow, so shall ye reap.' Your children have brought you what they reaped from their labours of love. I know you may not think it, but they killed those poor souls out of love for you. You don't have to worry about looking after these children, they're going to look after you. It was a shame those innocent people had to die, but they had certain things the Byrgen need to look after you. That's why I arranged for them to come here and then padlocked the gates."

The Byrgen had looked after him, but Jim didn't care for their idea of filial devotion. They'd torn open his stomach and inserted the umbilical cord, sealing up the wound with the pus that leaked from the holes in their chests. The pus formed huge green scabs of cadaveric matter and held the cord in place, but the pain and discomfort this caused Jim was unbearable.

To stop his screams they sealed up his mouth with the same pus, knitting his lips together with the stinking bitter substance, then his eyes, and nostrils. Jim panicked at this, he tried to claw at his face to break the pustular scabs, but they restrained him. He was terrified he was going to suffocate, but for some reason the umbilical cord meant he didn't.

The Byrgen surrounded him and their bodies began to meld and flow together. They formed themselves into a giant ovoid shape all around Jim. It was lined with the skins of their three other victims. They'd fashioned them into a single sac. Jim felt and heard all of this happen because he could no longer see.

Jim was glad of the scabs that filled his nostrils when the sac began to fill with a thick viscose liquid. Jim knew what the liquid was from the greasy, almost fibrous texture that flowed over his naked skin. It flooded the sac until he was floating in it.

From his work in the cemetery, attending to coffins that sometimes had to be moved, he knew what happened to a corpse after more than a month in a sealed container. The inner organs, the muscles and eventually even the skin, start to liquefy and form a thick rancid soup. That's what Jim was now suspended in, liquefied human remains.

RUN TO GROUND

He was back in the womb, just like he'd always fantasised. Only this womb wasn't like anything he'd longed for, it wasn't a place where life began, it was a hellish abomination filled with the products of the grave.

Jim had no idea how long he'd been in this womb, his only measure of time was the way things changed. The umbilical cord had grown and mutated over time, it was longer now, fatter and gnarled like a rotting vine. All manner of toxic things slid down it and were pumped into Jim's stomach. Things that writhed and thrashed inside him, squirming maggot-like things that nibbled away at his insides and made him curl up and spasm with the pain.

They were changing him, too. His body felt different, his skin had hardened and his arms and legs had grown and twisted themselves into new shapes. He was becoming something else inside this womb, something that would live much longer than a human being.

Jim heard a sharp rapping sound. He hadn't heard anything in a long time, except for the soft slithering of his surroundings. He realised someone was banging on the hardened earth on the outside of the womb.

There was more rapping, then he heard Father Powers' voice. "Jim, I know you can hear me, lad." Father Powers was talking to him in the womb, just like Duncan had done to his brother. His mother was wrong; you can be heard.

"Jim, just thought you'd like to know that the police have gone. They've attributed all three murders to you. Your photo's on the cover of all the tabloids. It took a lot of money, but we managed to keep St.

Dunstan's name out of this. There's a nationwide manhunt going on. Don't worry, they'll never find you down here, and by the time you come out you'll have changed beyond recognition.

"You're growing into something else entirely, that's what the Byrgen were for. You see, times are changing, it's getting harder to keep secrets these days, what with the internet and mobile technology. More and more people have heard the rumours about the heresy and some of them come snooping around here, asking about the scrolls. That's why we need another Byrfling to guard the tunnels. They've been too long without one. That's where you come in. That's what you're becoming.

"Say goodbye to your old self, lad. Jim Mcleod must die, so he can be reborn as something truly monstrous. Something that can guard ancient secrets. Something I'd be proud to have as a member of the family, not the cowardly scum you were before. I never had any sons. My wife died giving birth to our only child, a little girl. You were nearly a member of my family, only you weren't man enough to face up to your responsibilities. I lost my daughter when she left home and took her mother's maiden name. I never had a chance to make up with her because you drove my little girl to suicide when you ran out on her.

"That's right, lad, I'm Dawn's father."

THE END

"Run to Ground" is part of a story cycle known as *The Heresy Series*.

The series explores the ancient blasphemy known as the Qu'rm Saddic Heresy.

The following story "How the Dark Bleeds" is also part of this series, as is the novel *The Final Cut*, which is out now from Crystal Lake.

If you enjoy the two stories in this book then we think you'll also enjoy *The Final Cut*. In fact, we've included the first two chapters at the end of this book just to whet your appetite. Hope you enjoy.

For those who'd like to learn more about the Qu'rm Saddic heresy, we've also included a short essay by the leading academic expert on the heresy—Nicola Tanthus PhD.

HOW THE DARK BLEEDS

THE SCALPELS WERE so sharp Stephanie could almost taste them.

It had taken her a while to steal a full set. The long ones were the hardest to acquire. The surgeons notice when they go missing.

She arranged them in order of size for the tenth time that night, laying them out on the bare floor of the basement room. It used to be an auxiliary boiler room but they gutted it when they modernised the hospital's plumbing. Now it was empty apart from a few supply boxes. The bare walls hadn't been painted for over two decades and the only light bulb had been smashed.

Stephanie had brought a flashlight. She wasn't ready to let the darkness into the room. The darkness didn't threaten her, but what waited there did. Presences that thrived in the darkest hours and places.

The urge to use the scalpels was growing. Stephanie couldn't hold out much longer. She felt dizzy with longing as she picked up the shortest scalpel and thought about how it would feel slicing through her jugular.

Stephanie's heart beat faster and to hold back the

yearning just a little longer, she pressed her index finger onto the blade. It sliced through the layers of skin and a thick red trickle of blood ran out. She could feel the presences in the dark draw closer as she let the blood spatter on the concrete floor forming a tiny pool.

Stephanie shone the flashlight on the little red pool. Maybe it was because she hadn't eaten in a day or more, or perhaps she really was losing it, but Stephanie was sure she could see pictures reflected on the surface of the blood. Images that swam in and out of focus like sediment rising from the bottom of a disturbed pond.

The images looked familiar. She stared harder, willing them into focus as she realised what they were. They were scenes from her life. Not memories, because she was watching herself from the outside. It was a disconcerting feeling, like watching yourself on video, or hearing how your recorded voice sounds for the first time. Her life was being played back to her, stripped of all the self serving misconceptions that so often colour our memories.

There was a word for what she was experiencing but Stephanie couldn't quite remember it. She'd had a conversation about it just recently, she was sure. Maybe the images in the blood would remind her. She stared hard as a scene began to form, a scene from her recent past.

Stephanie saw herself on the hospital wards, in the ICU . . .

***

Stephanie's uniform hung awkwardly about her. She could never find one that fitted. They were always too small or too large for her.

HOW THE DARK BLEEDS

She tried to adjust it surreptitiously as the Duty Nurse briefed her. Stephanie nodded without paying too much attention. She was supposed to sit with someone on a suicide watch.

The patient had suffered third degree burns from a house fire. Her father had died in the fire and the patient had tried to take her own life, so she had to be kept under constant supervision.

Stephanie sat down beside the patient and smiled politely. The patient gave Stephanie a cursory glance and then went back to scowling at her book. She was thin, with close cropped brown hair, olive skin and elfin features. She seemed to be repressing an intense, twitchy energy, as though there were something inside her trying to scratch its way out.

Her right arm and shoulder were covered with heavy dressing. The dog eared paperback she was staring at was The Living Goddesses by Marija Gimbutas. There was a pile of similar textbooks and faded hardbacks by her bedside.

"Good book?" said Stephanie.

Without looking up the patient said: "Her work's largely dismissed by most academic and she makes too many unwarranted assertions, but her views on the origins of religion are worth consideration."

"But you're enjoying it, right?"

"This isn't the sort of book you read for enjoyment."

"No, I don't suppose it is. Are you a student then?"

The patient put down her book and stared straight ahead, not bothering to hide her irritation. "You know, none of the other nurses asked so many questions."

"I'm not like the other nurses."

The patient smiled and turned to look at Stephanie for the first time, gazing right into her. "No, you're not are you," she said, implying something Stephanie couldn't quite grasp.

"My name's Stephanie by the way, I didn't catch yours."

"It's Jan."

"Pleased to meet you. I'm sorry if I ask too many questions. I like to make time for people, that's all. The other nurses might be caught up with their workloads but I like to find out what's going on. You wouldn't believe the things I've seen, that they miss. The people that have just walked in here, right under their noses."

"Oh, I think I would."

Jan relaxed, and her mood thawed. "I'm not a student, but I was doing a PhD a few years ago. My Aunt brought my old books in. I'd left them at her house. She hopes I'll pick it up again, to take my mind off what happened."

"What did happen?"

"I'd rather talk about my PhD."

"Of course, sorry. I'm not an academic, but you could try explaining what it's about."

"Well it was supposed to be about 'Negative Depictions of Femininity in Pre-Rational Goddess Culture', or that was the title at least. It ended up being about the Heolfor."

"The what? Is that a foreign word or something?"

"It's ancient Anglo Saxon. It means gore, or blood spilled in anger, but it might have a deeper meaning, one whose roots go back to an almost forgotten myth." Jan pulled an old book out of the pile by her bed and turned to a passage. The print was too small for Stephanie to read. "The first definite mention of the myth is in the Nine Herbs Charm, an Old English spell to treat infection and poisoning. It says 'These nine herbs have power against nine horrors, against nine venoms and against nine poisons: Against the red venom, against the running venom, against the blood that walks in woman's form, in sisterhood compact.'"

"Okay, you're beginning to lose me."

"That's okay, I'm not done yet. There are a few other mentions in Anglo Saxon writing, including suggestions that the Heolfor were around before even the Celts got here. The next important reference to the Heolfor is in the Malleus Maleficarum."

Jan rifled through another book and pointed out a replica of a woodcut title page. "It's Latin for 'Hammer of the Witches.' Basically it's a handbook for hunting and persecuting witches written in 1486. At one point it tells the story of Marie Van Stratten, a woman who claimed her blood was bewitched and was desperate to be free of her so it could join the Heolfor. She claimed her blood was speaking to her and begging her to slash her wrists so it could escape her body. She disappeared soon after on the night of a new moon."

"Why a new moon?"

"Ah, now this is where it gets interesting. Have you heard of Edward Kelley?"

Stephanie smiled to herself and turned away so that Jan wouldn't see. She poured a glass of water so Jan wouldn't wonder why she'd moved. Some patients could be so taciturn to begin with, but get them on the right topic and they'll pour their hearts out.

"You should drink this," she said handing Jan the

glass. "Your throat sounds dry. Should I have heard of Edward Kelley?"

"Not necessarily," said Jan, putting down the water without touching it. "He was an alchemist and a spirit medium who hung out with Dr John Dee, Queen Elizabeth I's court magician. They used to speak to angels by scrying."

"Scrying?"

"Basically, Kelley used to stare at a polished black stone till he had visions. These angels would speak to him and Dr Dee would write down what they said. One of the things the angels told them about was . . . "

"Let me guess—the Heolfor."

"Give the lady a gold star. According to Dee and Kelley, the Heolfor represent the worst aspects of femininity and are governed by the dark side of the lunar goddess Monanom. She was a strange minor deity, a bit like the Roman god Juno. A lot of goddesses have like a threefold aspect, they're both a maiden, a mother and a crone, representing the three stages of a woman's life . . . I'm not boring you, am I? I have a tendency to go on a bit about this stuff."

"No, no, it's really interesting, carry on."

"Okay, so Monanom only has two aspects, the maiden and the crone, and they're joined back to back like Siamese twins. The maiden is in love with the sun god but she has to hide the dark crone from him. For this reason, her love is a chaste love and everyone sees her as the ideal woman while her hidden sister has to live in darkness, hidden from the sun where she can work her evil deeds. Everyone hates and fears the crone but loves and worships the maiden."

"Yeah, I've got a sister like that, loved by everyone."

HOW THE DARK BLEEDS

"Thought you might," said Jan, giving her another penetrating look. Stephanie looked down at the floor, embarrassed and unnerved. Sensing this, Jan flicked to another page in her book.

"So, anyway, the maiden aspect of Monanom inspires women to be faithful daughters, wives and mothers. The crone lives in darkness, she's strongest when the moon is new or hidden and she inspires madness, betrayal and murder in women. The moon is supposed to affect the tides and the blood, especially menstrual blood. So the crone's servants, the Heolfor, are composed of blood, because that's what she has most control over."

"So, they're like vampires then?"

"No, vampires feed on blood, the Heolfor are made entirely out of blood and nothing else. Or as Dr Dee wrote 'blood that taketh on the human form and walks as to a woman's carriage.' They were said to bewitch the blood with their song and drive people to hideous acts in the darkest hour of the night. Some scholars have suggested that this is the origin of the concept of 'bad blood' and also why early physicians were so keen on bloodletting to release bad humours."

"You have read a lot about this haven't you?"

"Told you I was obsessed."

"Were there lots of these Heolfor?"

"There were nine. That was an important and magical number to the Anglo Saxons. Each of the Heolfor represent a different type of aberrant female behaviour, a bit like Jungian archetypes, if you know about that."

"A little."

"There was one that represented the worst type of

wife, for instance, one who betrayed her husband, slept with his enemy and had him killed. Or the worst kind of mother, who slaughters her child, the worst daughter who disobeys and murders her father. That sort of thing. This doesn't freak you out, does it? A lot of people get all funny when I talk about it."

"No, not at all, it actually makes a lot of sense to me, strangely."

"Excuse me," said the Duty Nurse. She was standing right next to the bed holding a clipboard, but Stephanie hadn't seen her come up. "I've just been going through the staff roster and I can't seem to find you . . ."

***

Stephanie closed her eyes to stop the vision. She didn't want to see anymore. The rest of the memory was tedious and she was happy to let it end there.

So scrying was the word she was looking for. Was that what she was doing with the blood? Stephanie wasn't seeing any angels though. She wondered if Edward Kelley ever saw dark visions from his past. Things he hadn't told Dee about.

She stretched her back and shifted onto her haunches because her knees were sore. The flashlight flickered, its beam dimmer. The batteries were starting to go. She couldn't hold the dark at bay much longer.

She couldn't keep her eyes off the pool of blood either. Stephanie leant forward and gazed at it. An image of her reflection swam to the surface. Only it wasn't Stephanie's reflection as she was now, it was a reflection from the past. A transparent reflection in the window of a ward. A window through which Stephanie was watching Mike . . .

HOW THE DARK BLEEDS

***

He had his back to her and he seemed worn down, stooped and a little older. Stephanie couldn't stop herself feeling a twinge of satisfaction. Maybe if he hadn't left Stephanie for her own sister he might not be so sad.

Stephanie had been three months pregnant when Mike left. She miscarried soon after. It had happened at three in the morning. Stephanie had phoned Mike as she sat on the loo, screaming at him as the blood poured out of her. Mike had claimed he was at his mother's at the time, the liar.

Stephanie felt mean going over those memories though. Mike was looking at his child in an incubator. The tiny infant boy was six weeks premature. Mike had a right to be sad and concerned. Anyone in his position would be.

Stephanie usually avoided the Neonatal ICU. Today she'd decided to visit. She hadn't expected to see Mike here. She hung back, uncertain of what to do, not wanting to make things awkward.

Mike looked lonely. Her sister was nowhere to be seen. That was probably just as well. Stephanie didn't think she could face her at the moment.

Stephanie's sister had plotted against Stephanie her whole life. She made a point of stealing what Stephanie prized most, especially when she was a teenager, that's when her sister stole their parents' love. She'd been having mental problems and they had to take her out of school for a while.

Stephanie spent long hours in her bedroom, wearing the same nightie for weeks on end, listening to her sister play up to her parents downstairs. She was

65

being the perfect daughter that Stephanie could never be. Her parents never looked at her sister with the same weary disappointment they reserved for Stephanie.

It would make Stephanie so angry that she'd scream at her mother when she came in to change the bed sheets or try to coax Stephanie into a clean nightie. Her mother and father responded to these fits with a tired resignation.

Stephanie knew her sister was making the most of the situation. Soaking up the extra love and attention until finally there was none left for Stephanie.

Things got a little better when her sister went away. That's when Stephanie started taking her pills and seeing a psychiatrist. Sometimes she would tell her psychiatrist how she felt when she pictured her sister at boarding school or travelling in Europe. Stephanie's psychiatrist would always try and discourage her from thinking or talking about her sister, though. So Stephanie never told how she fantasised that her sister and seven others were secretly plotting her downfall.

Mike also discouraged Stephanie when she told him about her sister. He encouraged Stephanie not to dwell on her or what happened in her past. Then one day, without any warning he just up and left Stephanie for the one person who had stolen everything from her.

After what seemed like ages staring at the incubator, Mike turned round without any warning, and caught Stephanie's eye. Stephanie froze. She couldn't just turn her back and walk away. She had to face him. He was wearing the same look of weary resignation that she used to see on her parents' faces.

That was her sister's doing. That's how she made everyone look at Stephanie, eventually.

Mike stepped out into the corridor where Stephanie had been watching him. He hadn't shaved in a couple of days, there were streaks of gray running through his dark brown hair and his deep brown eyes looked watery and bloodshot. He appeared to have shrunk as well. He was never tall at five foot nine, but with everything weighing on his slumped shoulders he seemed to have lost two inches in height. Stephanie hoped her sister was happy.

"Stephanie . . . I . . . " Mike said, letting the sentence just trail off as though there were so many things he wanted to say that he couldn't pick one.

"How is he?" said Stephanie, pointing to the incubator.

"Haven't you been in to check yourself?" said Mike. "When was the last time you looked?"

"Look, Mike, please, I don't want to argue with you. I understand how you feel. I don't want to add to your grief." Mike looked surprised. "You understand how I feel?"

"Well obviously. Do you think I'm stupid?"

"No, no, of course not." Mike's tone changed. He became more conciliatory. "That's good. It's really good that you understand, it's a good sign." A tentative affection crept across Mike's face and he reached out and took Stephanie's hand.

Stephanie hadn't felt his fingers wrapped around hers for such a long time, it was a shock. She felt both joy and loss at the same time. Sometimes the simplest displays of emotion are the most honest. Stephanie's defences melted and she remembered why she loved

Mike and how fierce that love was, in spite of everything he'd done.

"Stephanie, could you . . . could you do something for me?"

"Of course," said Stephanie. Mike pointed to the incubator. "Something that would really help him, and me . . . and your parents." Stephanie began to feel uneasy at the mention of her parents. Her unease only grew as Mike reached into his pocket and she heard a familiar rattle.

Mike pulled out a bottle of pills. "Please start taking your medication again." Maybe it was because he reminded Stephanie how her parents tried to cajole and control her. Or maybe it was because he had taken complete advantage of her emotions, but Stephanie lost it. She knocked the bottle out of Mike's hand and it shattered as it hit the wall, scattering capsules all over the floor.

"Fuck you," she shouted. "You had me feeling something for you and you threw it back in my face. Stop making this my problem. I'm sorry for what's happened Mike, but you left me for my own sister. Stop trying to dope me with tranquilisers because you hurt me!"

Stephanie turned to leave and Mike grabbed her wrist to stop her. "Stephanie, I've spoken with Dr Connor and your parents . . . " Stephanie tried to punch Mike in the chest to make him let go. He held up his palm and caught her punch.

"Fuck you," she cried again.

"Stephanie please, you're in danger, great danger . . . "

***

Stephanie put her hands over her eyes and pushed her

head back so she didn't have to watch anymore. The blood was playing with her. It knew she didn't want to see these things.

Even though she knew how each scene ended, she couldn't stop looking. She couldn't tear her gaze away until the very last moment. There were things she didn't want to admit to, not yet.

The blood was aware of this, it had to be, it came from her body. Was it playing with her? Did it need her to admit something before it . . . before it . . . Stephanie didn't want to finish that thought either.

She was trapped between things she didn't want to remember and things she didn't want to think. Her eyes dropped back to the pool of blood. Another image was forming. She was in uniform again and back in the ICU . . .

***

Stephanie hadn't been back to the ICU since her run-in with the Duty Nurse. She'd found it was best to steer clear of certain parts of the hospital sometimes until things cooled down and the staff forgot about you.

Stephanie preferred to fly below the radar and not draw too much attention to herself. There was always something to keep you busy on the wards so it was easy to blend into the hospital without being bothered.

All the same, Stephanie had to risk the ire of the Duty Nurse to come back and check on Jan. She'd seen a lot of patients in distress while she'd been in the hospital. She knew many nurses remained detached and kept a professional distance. But you can't stop everyone from getting under your skin, you wouldn't be a good nurse if you did.

Stephanie was shocked when she saw Jan. She wasn't just slumped against the pillows propping her up, she'd sunk into them. Jan seemed to have lost an alarming amount of weight. Her skin was the colour of wax, and there were dark rings under her eyes. Her short hair was matted into brown clumps which stuck to her forehead with sweat. Her dressing had been changed but it was stained with perspiration.

Though she was hardly moving and just staring straight ahead of her, Jan still had that same twitchy energy, if anything it seemed to have intensified. The vein in her temple was bulging and throbbing, all of Jan's veins were. It was like they were alive, writhing under skin so pale it was almost transparent.

Stephanie drew the curtains around Jan's bed and sat down. Jan barely registered her presence. "Oh," she said, after a considerable pause. "It's you." She hardly moved her head, just flicked her eyes in Stephanie's direction. "Is everything okay?" Stephanie said. Jan rolled her eyes and sighed. "Does it look okay?"

"No, I suppose not. Have there been complications with your burns. Did you get infected?"

"Not from my burns, they're not the problem."

"I'm not sure I follow you?"

"Really? You were my last hope. I thought you, of all people, might have understood, considering what you know."

"Jan, you're not making any sense. If you know you've got an infection you've got to tell the doctors, otherwise they can't give you the treatment you need."

"There's no treatment for what I've got."

"It's not A.I.D.S, is it? Because you have to tell the

doctors about that. You could be putting other patients at risk."

Jan's chest started to quiver and her breath sped up. Stephanie thought she was about to have a coughing fit but then she realised Jan was actually laughing. "Oh Christ, you're in so much denial aren't you, it's so incredible it's almost endearing."

Stephanie bridled at this. "What do you mean? You think I'm in denial? I'm not the one hiding things from my doctors. You've got to tell them what's wrong with you if you've got an infection."

"They won't believe me if I tell them what's infecting me."

"Why on earth not? What is infecting you?" Jan turned to look at Stephanie for the first time since she'd come to see her. Her emaciated features made her eyes stand out, accentuating her piercing glare. "What did we talk about last time?"

"Last time I sat with you? It was your PhD wasn't it? Moon goddesses, witch hunting and that guy Edward something or other . . . "

"Kelley."

"Yes, that's right."

"And what else?" Stephanie searched her memory. "Oh yes, the Anglo Saxon myth about the thingies—the heel . . . erm helio . . . ?"

"Heolfor."

"Of course, I'm sorry, it's not a name I'm familiar with, so it's hard to recall."

"Not after you know what I know it's not. Then it gets right into your blood."

"Jan, I'm sorry I'm not as clever as you, with your PhD and everything, but you're talking in riddles and

I can't follow you. Has this got something to do with when you got burned, how you lost your father and tried to . . . erm . . . "

"Kill myself?"

"Yes, I err . . . I wasn't trying to be insensitive."

"Perish the thought."

"Do you want to talk about it? Will that help?"

"Help me or you?"

"I'm not sure what you mean—help you of course."

"I'm beyond help now."

"Don't talk that way."

"Okay, then let's talk about the Heolfor." Jan made a feeble gesture towards the books that lay unopened by her bedside. "My reading only scratched the surface of the myth. Most of my research was done in the field. I wanted to get a proper sense of where these beliefs came from. Why people needed to hold them. There are no precedents in other pagan religions."

"Really?"

"Oh yes, according to Austin Osman Spare, he's a 20th century artist and mystic, the idea of a being made entirely of blood is unique to Ancient Britain. Spare called them 'a living blood sacrifice, bound to the service of the moon's dark designs. A sinister sisterhood devoted to delirium and deviltry'."

"So how on earth do you do fieldwork on something like that?"

"You have to know where the Heolfor congregate and how such a sisterhood was said to manifest in these places."

"Places like what?"

"Anywhere blood is spilt and people take leave of their senses in the darkest hours, a battlefield, a site of slaughter and atrocity, even a hospital."

"Like this one?"

"Wasn't it you who told me about the things that take place here, right under the noses of people too busy to see them?"

"You did field research right here, in this hospital?"

"Did you know it's built on the site of the last great Pagan uprising in Britain? King Sighere of Essex and his army of followers were put to the sword here in 683 on the orders of Augustine of Canterbury, the Pope's emissary and the first Archbishop of Canterbury."

"How can you possibly know that?"

"There was an archaeological dig here when they laid the foundations for the hospital. They found all the bones, along with some pagan artefacts. Some of it's still on display at the local museum. But that's not all, in the eighteenth century they built one of the first British asylums here. It was burned to the ground in 1793 when the inmates rebelled and beheaded all the trustees with a makeshift guillotine in solidarity with the French Reign of Terror. This has long been a site of death and destruction, of dark, dark places that never lose the stain of delirium. What better place to search for the Heolfor."

"But you said they were a myth, right? You're talking as if they're real. I mean, you can't actually see a mythical being can you?"

Jan went very quiet at this and stared intently up at the ceiling. "I'm sorry," said Stephanie after a long pause. "I didn't insult you did I?"

"You asked me why I didn't tell the doctors about my infection. This is why. You're the only person in this hospital who might understand what's happened to me, and even you find it hard to believe."

"Okay, I didn't say I didn't believe you, but I'm not actually sure what you're talking about. How can I believe you when you hide what you mean behind all these riddles?"

"You're right, it's a trust issue. People think I'm crazy enough without finding out the truth. That's why I keep them at bay with riddles."

"And to show them how clever you are."

"Well there is that."

"Please tell me what happened, I won't judge you."

"I wouldn't be so sure about that."

"You can trust me." Stephanie placed her hand on Jan's.

After another pause, Jan said, "I've seen them—the Heolfor, right here in this hospital."

"You've seen them, where?"

"In the basement, there's an abandoned storage room, it's right over the spot where they found all the bones from the massacre. There's no light down there, which is why they like it. I studied the schematics of the hospital, I snuck in on a new moon and I went looking for them. There's things about them I didn't know, though."

"What sort of things?"

"They're not immortal, they can die over time and they need new blood to replenish their ranks. They sang to me."

"Sang?"

"Stood around me in a circle and sang, seven of them."

"I thought you said there were nine."

"I told you they need to replenish their ranks, that's why they sang, it's how they infected me."

HOW THE DARK BLEEDS

"By singing?"

"Directly to my blood. They converted it, harmonised it I suppose, made it one of them. Now it isn't part of me. It's fighting me to get out. Every time my heart beats my blood screams to be free, begs me to open up my veins, so it can be rid of me and join its sisters. That's why I'm on suicide watch."

"You think your blood wants you to kill yourself."

"Not kill myself, though I will die if it gets its way. It wants to leave me, to become something else, something deranged and malevolent, a blood being aligned to the darkness."

"What can you do?"

"I tried to fight back but I ended up here. Do you know what it's like to feel your blood turn against you, to develop thoughts of its own? To know that it's plotting your death as it moves through your body. I couldn't give in to it so I decided to poison it. I was walking in the woods near my home and I found a rotting badger. I picked it up, took it home and stuck a kitchen knife in it. My plan was to stick the knife in my body and give myself septicaemia. If I poisoned my blood then I'd kill the blood being, deny the Heolfor their new sister. I was standing at the kitchen sink with the rotting beast when my dad came in. We still share a house. He saw what I was about to do and he tried to get the knife off me. He probably thought I was having another of my episodes. I've had problems on and off since my mother died when I was twelve, that's why I still live with him.

"He nearly took the knife off me, but he's getting weak and old and I was angry. Angry that he'd try to prolong my suffering, try to stop me killing what was festering in my veins. So I lunged at him, instead. He didn't expect that, and the knife went straight into his chest. I remember the tiny 'clunk' the handle made as it hit his ribs. How he coughed and gurgled as the blood from his lung caught in his throat. He stepped backwards and reached for the kitchen counter to steady himself, but he missed it and toppled over backwards.

"He reached out to me as he was lying there, slumped against the dishwasher. 'Jan love,' he said. 'For God's sake, please . . . call an ambulance . . . please . . .' I looked at him lying there, crumpled pathetic and bleeding. This wasn't the man who'd raised me since my mother died. Who'd sat with me when I got ill, comforted me when I was sad and put a roof over my head. This was a vulnerable old man who'd just been infected with septicaemia. So I pulled the knife out of his chest and I rammed it into his left eye. He kicked a few times, went into spasms then he lay still. It was a mercy killing, that's what I told myself. Septicaemia is a hell of a way to die and I'd just saved him from that.

"I felt really cold after that. I couldn't stop shivering or keep my hands steady. I knew I had to hide the evidence and I knew I had to get back to this hospital. So I went to the garage and I got a can of petrol, then I doused the house and set a match to it."

Jan held up her bandaged arm. "That's how I got this. I think I was cutting off all ties to my past life, limiting my options so I couldn't avoid the inevitable. A neighbour called an ambulance and they took me here, like I knew they would. It's a new moon tomorrow night. I don't have much longer. I can't fight my own blood anymore. A policeman came to see me this morning, full of questions and insinuations. It won't be long till they find out what really happened. But I won't be around to face them."

Stephanie had no idea what to say. Jan's story had knocked the wind out of her, like a blow to the solar plexus. "You told me I could trust you," said Jan. "Well, I have. I don't think you'll judge me either because I think I know what you're planning to do. Even if you don't yet . . ."

***

Stephanie winced at the pain shooting through her palm. She looked away from the blood to her hand and saw that she'd stabbed herself with the scalpel to stop the vision. How much longer could she struggle with the blood before she gave in and saw what it really wanted to show her?

More blood trickled from her palm. She held her hand over the tiny pool and let the fresh blood add to it. It ran along her palm and down the length of her thumb, dripping from the tip into the pool.

Stephanie sighed, the release she felt was almost orgasmic. Her heart beat faster in anticipation, spurred on by the blood pushing its way through the organ. It sang in her ears, rising in volume as each drop joined the pool.

Stephanie's eyes drifted back to the pool as the drips rippled its surface, churning up new visions. She saw herself in a different part of the hospital. She was carrying a tray with blood samples on it . . .

***

The samples came from the children's Oncology and Haematology ward. They'd been taken from a child with MRSA. More tests were needed and a doctor had

77

asked Stephanie to run the samples up to be despatched. As soon as she was away from the ward she knew what she was going to do. It was as if the doctor had handed her the plan along with the tray, it was that inevitable.

She stopped to pick up a fresh syringe and headed down to the Neonatal ICU. With the recent cutbacks, it wasn't always fully staffed and during a shift change it could be unattended for up to twenty minutes. This was all the time Stephanie needed.

She stood over the incubator and gazed at her sister's child. She thought of the poor thing growing up in her sister's care. A woman who had robbed Stephanie of everything she'd loved. If this was the way she treated Stephanie, her own flesh and blood, then how much worse would she treat her own son?

Stephanie considered the abuse and neglect she'd suffered at her sister's hand. She couldn't let this innocent child fall victim to that. What sort of life would he have with that woman as his mother? Much better to show him mercy now than to inflict years of mistreatment on him.

He was so tiny and so frail, barely aware he was even alive. Would it be such a crime to take something from someone who hardly knew what they had? Especially if you were saving him from so much misery. He came from her bloodline; she couldn't turn her back on him.

Stephanie took the syringe out of the wrapper and filled it from the phial of infected blood. Her hands shook as she did.

She opened the incubator and stroked the head of the tiny boy inside. His eyes weren't able to open yet but he stirred and reached out for her. His fingers were so small they couldn't properly clasp Stephanie's little finger.

"Shh," Stephanie said. "It's okay, it will all be over soon." She pinched his little thigh until she saw a vein. He wriggled and let out a barely audible sigh of complaint, but she held him still and stuck the needle in his vein then pushed down the plunger.

Stephanie heard footsteps in the corridor. She quickly closed the incubator and left the room, dropping the syringe and the other blood samples in the bin on the way out. "God speed little man," she said over her shoulder and hurried out of the neonatal ICU.

Stephanie wasn't certain what to do with herself once it was all over. She felt a sudden need to speak about it, to unburden herself. She realised there was only one person to whom she could talk.

Stephanie went to look for Jan, but when she got to the ICU her bed was empty. She asked one of the nurses on duty where Jan was but no one knew. The nurse said there was a shortage of beds so Jan had probably been moved to another part of the hospital.

Stephanie went back to the bed. All of Jan's books were still there so she couldn't have been moved. She asked around the other patients in the ward and none of them had seen Jan all day.

Stephanie began to get worried. She flicked through Jan's books to see if she could find anything that might give her a clue as to where Jan might be. She scanned the pages and the indexes, looking for any reference to the Heolfor, but she couldn't find one. The only mention of the word she found was in a collection of Anglo Saxon poetry which gave a brief translation of the word as: 'blood or gore'.

Stephanie remembered what Jan had said about encountering the Heolfor in the basement and decided that's where she must be. She made her way straight to the stairs.

The basement was musty. It didn't have the same sterile, disinfected smell as the rest of the hospital. The service corridors were like a low-ceilinged maze. There was a constant throb and hum from the back-up generators.

It was more by accident that Stephanie found the door to the subbasement and made her way down the stairs. There was only one light, flickering in the corridor. Luckily, the hours she'd spent in darkened rooms as a teenager meant Stephanie had great night vision and her eyes quickly adjusted to the dark.

Stephanie turned a corner at the end of the corridor into complete darkness. She stumbled on with her arms outstretched until her eyes adjusted and she made out a door up ahead. As she reached for the handle the temperature seemed to plummet, as if the blood had drained from her body. At the same time Stephanie could hear a high pitched whistling in her ears.

The room on the other side of the door smelled of copper and salt. Stephanie was reminded of the taste of old pennies under the tongue. In the centre of the room was what looked like a discarded white sack. As Stephanie peered closer she saw that it was Jan's naked body.

Jan's throat and wrists had been slashed open. The cuts were deep and the edges ragged and tattered.

HOW THE DARK BLEEDS

Jan's blood had pooled in a thick red puddle in front of her. Stephanie blinked when she saw something rising out of the puddle. It looked at first like long thin drips were running out of the puddle towards the ceiling, as though gravity had been reversed.

The drips were forming themselves into long, thin shapes. The shapes were sinuous and began to intertwine themselves, branching out like tiny underwater fronds as they formed a larger structure.

The structure seemed to be sucking all the blood from the puddle as it formed itself. The rivulets of blood were making the outline of a body, like a wireframe image. No, not a wireframe image, it was like a life-sized map of the human circulatory system forming itself right in front of Stephanie.

Stephanie could see all the veins and arteries of a human body, of Jan's body, as the figure turned to regard her. It had no eyes, just the capillaries that would have flowed through an eyeball.

Stephanie recognised something of Jan in the hideous stare of this blood being. What she saw was the personification of Jan's unhinged fury. The deranged anger that had pushed a knife, soaked in rotting blood, into her father's chest, then killed him as he begged her for help.

Dark red stains were appearing on the walls and the floor around Stephanie. At first, the stains looked ancient but, as they spread, they began to get fresher and fresher. Blood oozed into them to form pools. Sinuous, living veins and arteries snaked out of the blood pools and formed themselves into more living circulatory systems.

There were eight of them now, including the blood being that had once been Jan. Each of them seemed to represent a different type of malevolent delirium. Destruction, madness and denial throbbed in the living veins that composed their bodies.

They formed a circle around Stephanie and opened their wet, red mouths to sing. The sound they made was the high pitched whine of blood whistling in the ears coupled with the whoosh and the roar as it pumps through the heart.

Stephanie held her hands up to her ears and fell to her knees. It did no good. She couldn't block out their song. They weren't singing to her. They were singing to her blood.

Infecting it. Altering it. Converting it. Until it was one with them . . .

***

That had been a month ago. The images Stephanie saw in the blood sped up.

***

She saw herself suffering as her blood rebelled against her. As it developed its own consciousness and became an alien entity inside her. Stephanie's heart pumped the blood through her veins but it was no longer a part of her.

Stephanie could feel her blood plotting against her as it circulated round her body. It longed to be free of her, to shuffle off her flesh and bones and take its true form. The vital fluid that gave her life ached to be rid of her, yearned to leave her and join its unholy sisters. Every time she saw a vein throb or an artery stand out on her skin Stephanie knew what her blood was planning.

She fell in love with sharp objects. Ached with

longing when she saw a knife. Stephanie became so desperate to feel a blade slice through her veins she would shake whenever she held one. Her heart would beat faster and her blood would sing of release. That's why she stole and collected all the scalpels.

Stephanie knew she wouldn't be able to hold out past the next new moon. Her blood was wearing her down. The only thing that gave her the strength to resist was the knowledge of what a monstrous thing it wanted to become. Then she'd think about what she did to her sister's child and realise she was already monstrous herself.

The child died a few weeks later and the ensuing investigation pointed to Stephanie. With the net closing in on her, she gathered up her scalpels and a flashlight and decamped to the basement.

***

Kneeling on the floor, Stephanie stared at the image in the blood, and saw herself. The cycle had come around to the beginning. Only this time she wouldn't be allowed to look away. This time she would have to face what the blood was trying to show her.

Stephanie saw why the Duty Nurse had no record of her that first time she met Jan and why none of the nurses' uniforms fitted her.

She saw Mike hold her wrist as she tried to punch him and he said "Stephanie please, you're in danger, great danger. You're suffering from postpartum psychosis. You came off your pills because you didn't want to endanger our child, remember? Like you did last time, when you miscarried."

"Let me go," Stephanie said, trying to pull away. "I've got to get back to my rounds."

83

"Stephanie you don't work in the hospital. You've been stealing uniforms and posing as a nurse. You're going to get into real trouble if you don't stop."

"Lies. You're lying. This is all my sister's doing. First she steals you from me, then she poisons your mind against me."

"No one stole me away from you Stephanie. You don't have a sister. You've never had a sister. You're an only child! This is all part of your delusion. It's why you've got to start back on your medication. You're a danger to yourself and . . . and . . . "

***

Mike couldn't bring himself to finish that sentence, but he didn't need to. Stephanie had proven him right. It was her own child she'd killed.

Stephanie had a completely different life inside her now. It was time to give birth to it. The scalpels could not cut her anywhere near as deeply as the truth had. That was why the blood had shown her—so she could be ready.

Stephanie made a fist with her left hand so the veins stood out on her wrist and bent her hand back so she could see the artery. Then she took a scalpel and made a deep incision, cutting down from the forearm towards the wrist.

Stephanie felt a roar of joy inside her as the blood gushed out in rhythmic spurts. She took the scalpel in her left hand and repeated the process. It was more painful this time. The fingers on her left hand were numb from blood loss and she couldn't cut so accurately.

She felt cold, bitterly cold and empty. Coloured blotches appeared in front of her eyes and she fought dizziness.

HOW THE DARK BLEEDS

Stephanie picked up a longer scalpel. It wasn't easy. Her fingers felt like balloons and were slick with escaping blood. She lifted the scalpel to her throat.

The blood inside her carotid artery was so desperate to get out that the whole artery was throbbing and distended. Stephanie didn't have to search for it.

She plunged the tip of the scalpel directly into the artery and sliced down. The blood escaped in an ecstatic red spray like a fine mist.

The flashlight flickered and finally died. Stephanie fell forward and ceased to exist.

***

The new life fled Stephanie's body like an insane notion. It pooled into a glorious red delirium as the darkness crept in and the others joined her.

She rose up corpuscle by corpuscle into the murderous frenzy of her new self. She was slick and red and fluid and entirely without tissue or bone.

Her eight companions were waiting to greet her. The mad murderous sisters she'd fantasised about her whole life. The siblings who had plotted Stephanie's downfall, just as she'd always known they would.

"How The Dark Bleeds" was first published in the collection *STUCK ON YOU AND OTHER PRIME CUTS* from Crystal Lake Publishing.

I BET YOU DIDN'T SEE THAT COMING, GENTLE READER. SOMETIMES IT'S NOT JUST THE PAST THAT REMAINS BURIED OR OUR SINS THAT WILL FIND US OUT.
AND BECAUSE I KNOW THAT'S ONLY WHETTED YOUR APPETITE AND YOU'RE CLAMOURING FOR MORE, I HAVE ANOTHER STORY FOR YOU -- HOW THE DARK BLEEDS.
THIS ONE ALSO CONCERNS THE QU'RM SADDIC HERESY, AS DOES THE SCHOLARLY ARTICLE THAT ROUNDS OUT OUR BOOK.
YOU MAY BE WONDERING WHY YOUR DEAR OLD UNCLE JASP IS SO GOOD TO YOU. LET'S JUST SAY I LOST MY HEAD. WELL, I HAD TO FIND SOME WAY TO GET THIS STICK OUT OF MY BUTT!
Moran

The Qu'rm Saddic Heresy
by Nicola Tanthus PhD,
Associate Professor, Camford University

The Qu'rm Saddic Heresy, also known as the 'Faith that Comes Before Man' and the 'Oldest Truth,' is one of those enigmatic by-roads travelled by scholars of antiquity, especially those interested in lost and ancient beliefs. As with other heretics such the Gnostics, the Bogomils and the Cathars, most of what we know about the heresy comes from its harshest critics. But whereas many works have come to light, in the case of Gnosticism, that allow the heretics to speak to us across the ages, no document has yet been discovered that belongs to this heretical set of beliefs. Though the ancient Greek scholar, Achaikos of Thebes, informs us its adherents claimed all religious beliefs stem from this heresy and are a mere corruption of the more profound truths it contains.

This belief is mirrored in the writing of Italian scholar and Catholic priest Marsilio Ficino, who proposed the doctrine of the *Prisca Theologia*, which asserts that a single true theology exists, one that underlies all world religions, and was given by God to man in antiquity. Ficino, the first modern translator of both the *Corpus Hermeticum* and the works of Plato, never directly referred to the Qu'rm Saddic heresy in his writing. However, later commentators on his work have inferred certain references to it. Given the precarious political situation that Ficino operated in, and given that he was a proponent of pagan philosophers in a highly Christian power structure, it is not surprising that he would not make any direct reference to a heresy that, if the rumours are to be believed, has been brutally suppressed since religion became organised and allied to the state.[1]

Ficino's brilliant, but ultimately doomed disciple Giovanni Pico Mirandola is also said to have made veiled allusions to the Qu'rm Saddic heresy in his much feted *900 Theses* and his *Oration on the Dignity of Man.*[2] There are some that have hinted that Mirandola's mysterious death by poison at the young age of 31 may have been linked to the heresy. That other most famous Renaissance philosopher: Giordano Bruno, was also rumored to be in possession of certain scrolls that pertained to the ancient heresy. Given that Bruno was subsequently burned at the stake for heresy himself in February 17th, 1600, some fringe historians have speculated as to the truth of these rumours.[3]

Ficino, Mirandola and Bruno were scholars who rescued ancient pagan philosophies and made them available to early Enlightenment audiences. By the time they were doing this, the Qu'rm Saddic Heresy was already considered impossibly old. One of the earliest references we have to the heresy comes from the Ebla Tablets, 1800 clay cuneiform tablets found in the Syrian city of Ebla. The tablets speak of an incident in the Mesopotamian city of Harran, one of the oldest human settlements and the site of perhaps the world's

---

1. Yates, Frances *Giardano Bruno and the Hermetic Tradition* (1964) pp 15
    ISBN-10: 041527849X
2. Ibid
3. Lachman, Gary *The Quest for Hermes Trismegistus* (2011) pp 210, ISBN-
    13: 978-0863157981

first university, or centre of learning. Harran was linked to Elba due to the marriage of an Harranian city ruler to the Eblanian princess Zugalum.[4] Even when the tablets were written, the incident was said to be ancient history. It concerns the expulsion of a school of heretics, from the university, who were said to be misleading the student body with their blasphemous teachings. This is the first time the heresy is referred to as the Qu'rm Saddic heresy, though no explanation is given as to where this name originates. The heretics in question were summarily stoned to death.

Although I stated earlier that no actual texts outlining the beliefs of the heretics have survived, Johannes Hennenbloch, the 17th century Swiss scholar, claimed that the mysterious Voynich Manuscript was in fact a copy of a text central to the heresy. Dating to the 15th century, the manuscript was purchased by the Holy Roman Emperor Rudolph from Dr. John Dee in 1586. Believed to have been written by Roger Bacon, the volume contains many pages of an indecipherable text accompanying strange botanical and zodiacal drawings. No one has ever been able to decipher the writings but Hennenbloch makes an interesting argument for them being part of a lost cannon of the Qu'rm Saddic heresy.[5]

Subtle allusions to the heresy have appeared in many occult writings down through the ages. Most notably in the works of Christian Rosenkreuz and other Rosicrucians, then later in the writings of the Theosophists Madame Blavatsky and Rudolph Steiner as well as the mystic G. I Gurdjieff. Perhaps the most

---

4. Moorey, Peter Roger Stuart , A Century of Biblical Archaeology (1991), pp 149, ISBN 978-0-664-25392-9.
5. To view the Voynich manuscript and decide for yourself go to http://beinecke.library.yale.edu/collections/highlights/voynich-manuscript

interesting development in the history of the heresy was its adoption by weird fiction writers in the early 20th Century.

Little is known about the life of Herbert W. Soames, other than that he lived in Schenectady, and published in the pulp magazines of the early 20th century, most notably between 1919 to 1931. Many of his most salubrious and sensational stories featured references to the heresy that, in spite of their many literary faults, suggest the author had a knowledge of the more esoteric strands of the Qu'rm Saddic beliefs. Titles such as *Murder in the Name of Monanom, Blood for the Byrflings* and *My Heart Beats Fast for the Heolfor* thrilled readers of such forgotten publications as *Racy Tales, The Red Book* and *All Male Stories*.

In contrast, L.P. Hartington was a Don of the University of Camford, who in 1940 published a slim collection of stories entitled *Late in the Day it Came to Pass*. The stories are very much in the vein of M. R. James, Walter De La Mere and Lord Dunsany. While they lack the power and artistry of those same writers, one or two of them are eerily effective, especially the haunting and morose *Why the Willows Weep for Me*. All but two of the eight stories in the small volume deal in one way or another with concepts that are central to the Qu'rm Saddic heresy.

Both authors are long out of print. Soames's work was never collected, and Hartington's had a limited print run. As a consequence, the stories never appear online and are seldom to be found in the back catalogues of booksellers. If you do come across a copy of *Late in the Day it Came to Pass*, or a pulp containing Soames's work, be warned, despite their scarcity and novelty, their literary merits do not match the exorbitant prices that are asked for them.

In spite of the Western occult revival that began in the 1960s, the Qu'rm Saddic heresy was almost completely ignored by esoteric writers in the latter half of the 20th century. I am reliably informed, however, that it has recently come back into favour as a fictional theme in the early part of the 21st century. I have not read the works of such writers as L.L. Smith, Jasper Bark or Simone Lastwick, whose work is said to touch upon the heresy, but I am reliably informed that there is little there to recommend them, other than a macabre ingenuity and a tiny amount of scholarship.

What is most astonishing about the Qu'rm Saddic heresy, is that a belief system that was said to be old when our most ancient records were made, should still exert a hold on the contemporary imagination. There is an allure that surrounds forbidden truths and a certain mystique about banned beliefs. A sense of longing pervades their study, a yearning for deeper answers and a better glimpse into the darker matters of the cosmos.

This is perhaps why they inspire such frightful fiction (in both senses of the word). It's also why the unwary and the foolhardy seek to learn more about them. There is something within human nature that can't help but question the perceived wisdom of its age. That's why there will always be heretics and heresy, and why we seek out dark truths that may best be left to antiquity.

Crystal Lake Publishing would like to thank the author for her kind permission to reproduce this work.

Excerpted from:

The Final Cut
by
Jasper Bark

CHAPTER 1

SO, **LET ME** see if I've got this right," Ashkan paused for effect. Like a lot of gangsters, he fancied himself a bit of an actor. The Iranian Al Pacino was how he styled himself. Right now his well practised glare was boring a hole in Sam's forehead.

"You muppets borrowed fifty grand of my money, my fucking money, to shoot a feature film. Ten days you said, ten days to shoot it. Two months to edit it, then blam, stick it out on the net as video on demand and we'll recoup the cost in a matter of weeks. Am I lying?"

"No," said Sam, appalled at how high and frightened his voice sounded. "Look if you just give us a bit of time we can . . . "

Ashkan brought the back of his hand across Sam's face. The blow sent Sam sprawling and the only reason he didn't fall out of the chair was because he was held there with duct tape. The side of his face stung and it took a second for his vision to come back into focus.

"When it's your cue to fucking speak I'll tell you, alright?" said Ashkan. Sam nodded and his head throbbed. Ashkan drew himself up to his full height. At six five he was pretty imposing. He adjusted his leather jacket and smoothed down his Ben Sherman shirt like he was about to go on stage. Then he looked from Sam to Jimmy, who was duct taped to the chair next to him.

"See, what really disappoints me is, I like you guys. I like what you do. You're good at it. So I put in a little sweetener. I let you off the interest for six whole months. That should've been enough time to clear the whole debt. Now, some people might think I was going soft. But I saw it as an investment in my acting career. You guys were writing me a big part in the movie, so it was the least I could do. So yesterday, I rock up at the set with my crew, looking to show off me mad acting skills and what do I find, Farshad?"

"These two cunts, with their dicks in their hands and fuck all else," said Farshad, a short guy with a thick beard and huge shoulders. He was standing behind Sam and Jimmy.

"That's right," said Ashkan. "And trust me guys, as far as dicks go, they weren't that impressive. I was expecting lights, cameras, the whole fucking shebang. Instead I got mugged off. No equipment, no script, no fucking actors, just you two cunts in an empty fucking warehouse. That's all I got to show for my fifty grand. Am I lying?"

Sam and Jimmy shook their heads.

"You know what else I found out? Last week you two pissants tried to buy fifty grand's worth of coke from one of my rivals. One of my fucking rivals! Only someone pulled a gun as it was going down and you were left with fuck all to show for yourselves. What were you gonna do with all that coke? Sell it to your friends in the film biz?"

Sam and Jimmy looked at each other, then nodded hesitantly.

"So you never had any intention of making a film then?"

Sam didn't know what to do.

"You can talk now," said Ashkan.

"No, we're still going to make the film," said Sam. "I swear we're going to make it, but we had overheads. I maxed out all my cards funding our last feature and costs were spiralling. We were going to take the profits from the coke and plough it all back into the film, I swear to you we were."

"Whose idea was this?"

"It . . . it was mine," Jimmy croaked, after a long pause. He was sweating heavily, it ran in trickles from his chestnut curls and pooled in his beard. He blinked nervously.

"Jimmy thought we could use some of his underworld contacts and bring the deal off quickly," said Sam.

"Oh yeah," said Ashkan with a derisive snort. "Big man is Jimmy, really well connected. See, what I don't understand is, I just found you got some huge fucking trust fund waiting for you. So what the fuck you getting mixed up with all this shit for?"

Sam hung his head. "It's my parents," he said in a small voice.

"What?"

"It's my fucking parents. They won't let me access the fund until I get a proper job, in the City or something, raping third world countries."

"You have to admit they've got a point. I mean you wouldn't be in this mess if you had a proper job and I wouldn't be about to do this."

Ashkan clicked his fingers. Faisal, one of the thugs who'd grabbed Sam and Jimmy and driven them to the Bethnal Green lock up, sidled up to Ashkan. He was tall and rangy, with a thick black moustache and a scar down his left cheek. He handed Ashkan a syringe. It was the big, thick kind you find in hospitals, not the sort you get at a needle exchange. It was full of clear liquid.

Ashkan grabbed hold of Jimmy's hair and bent his head to one side. A blue vein throbbed on Jimmy's neck, Ashkan plunged the syringe into it.

"Jesus, Ashkan," Jimmy screamed, "What the fuck, what the fuck?"

"Just giving you a little taste innit," said Ashkan, pushing the plunger. "Thought you boys liked this sorta shit."

"The fuck is it?" Jimmy looked like he was going to have a fit. The muscles in his legs spasmed and his eyes twitched.

"This shit? This is better than meth, better than any of that crap you get on the street. This is from my private collection. Save it for special occasions, like this one." Ashkan clicked his fingers and one of his flunkies handed him another syringe.

"Please," said Sam, as Ashkan approached. "Not the neck, please."

"It's better in the jugular vein, innit. Goes straight to the brain see. Gives you twice the fucking hit— Blam!"

Sam felt a sharp prick as the needle hit his vein and the drug shot into his blood. His heart hammered like he was going into cardiac arrest and an ice cold wave washed over him. All the hairs on his body stood on end. The mother of all rushes charged through him. Ashkan hadn't lied, this stuff was powerful. Sam's head began to shake and his jaw worked involuntarily. He was blinking about a hundred times a minute.

Faisal put a laptop down on a card table in front of them. "Have I got your attention? Good. Wouldn't want you to miss a minute of this." Ashkan opened the laptop. "You boys like film shows don't you? Well I've got one mother of a film for you." He clicked an icon on the screen and a piece of footage came up. "See this? This is what happens when you fuck with me. When you take my money and mug me off in front of my crew." Ashkan patted Sam and Jimmy on the shoulders. "Enjoy the show boys."

The footage showed a dimly lit stone room that could have been a cellar or a prison cell. The camera, held by an amateur, swung unsteadily about the space. It picked out three figures, two men and a woman, strapped to operating tables which were covered in thick plastic sheeting.

One of the men was screaming and sobbing, snot streamed down his top lip as he writhed and fought his straps. The other man, from his expression, was bargaining for his life. He looked Mediterranean, but was shouting in a language that sounded Arabic.

The woman couldn't have been a bigger contrast. She lay very still, her body completely relaxed and her face serene. She seemed completely at peace with what was going to be done to her.

She was very striking, with strawberry blonde hair and high cheekbones. Her curves suggested a sensuous nature, but her eyes seemed to look heavenward, giving her a saintly, almost beatific look.

"This the tape you got from Mr Isimud?" said Farshad.

"Yeah man," replied Ashkan. "This is some seriously fucked up shit, seriously fucked up."

"Sweet, wanted to see this for ages."

"Some of the things they do man, they're like artists, trust me, artists—not killers." Ashkan smacked Sam and Jimmy on the back of the head. He reached over their shoulders and pointed at the screen. "Pay attention boys, this is my money back guarantee. I guarantee this will happen to you if I don't get my money back."

CHAPTER 2:

THE CAMERA PUSHED in to a close shot of the Mediterranean guy's face. He was still babbling desperately as two dark figures moved in on either side. The figures were blurry shadows, underlit and out of focus. Sam wasn't sure how they'd achieved the effect because the Mediterranean guy's face was crystal clear, so were the scalpels the figures held.

The blurry figures moved in unison, as though choreographed. They stretched a tight strap across the guy's forehead to keep his head still. Only his eyes rolled wildly as he pleaded for his life. Then the figures each took hold of an eyelid and pried them apart.

With their other hands the figures brought the scalpels down into the corners of the guy's eyes. Using tiny, deft movements they severed the muscle tissue holding his eyeballs in place. The guy stopped imploring the figures and shrieked with pain and fear.

Thin streams of blood spurted from the guy's eye sockets. The figures put down their scalpels and each produced a set of forceps. They took hold of his eyeballs with the forceps and lifted them out of their sockets, pulling them as far as their optic nerves would stretch. Next they turned the eyeballs so the pupils were pointed at the guy's mouth. Working together, as though their free hands belonged to the same body, the figures applied dental clamps to the guy's mouth and forced his jaws apart, holding his eyeballs over his mouth the whole while.

With the clamps in place, the figures picked up their scalpels again and took to slicing off the guy's top and bottom lips. Blood sprayed the cornea of one eyeball and Sam realised that, as the optic nerves were still attached, the guy could still see out of his severed eyes. He was being forced to watch an extreme close up of his own mutilation.

When the lips were removed, the hand of one figure produced a tiny chisel and held it over the guy's front tooth. It was the sort of delicate tool a sculptor would use to apply the finishing touches to a marble bust. The other figure's hand brought a mallet into shot.

The camera pushed in to a close up of the guy's open mouth and throat. The mallet struck the chisel on his front tooth, with such swift force, that the tooth was not only knocked out of its gum, it embedded itself in the lining of the guy's throat.

The guy choked and yelled in agony, his throat going into spasms. The figures continued to knock his teeth out, angling the chisel with such precision, and striking it with such power, that each of the teeth was driven into a different part of the guy's throat. When they were done the whole of his gullet was raw and torn and lined with teeth.

"Jesus this is fucking hardcore," said Farshad. "Is this for real?"

"Dunno," said Ashkan. "Ain't seen this bit before."

EXCERPT FROM *THE FINAL CUT*

"Thought you said you'd watched it all the way through? Twice now."

"I have, I just ain't seen this bit before. Must be some glitch or something."

The camera pulled back from the ruined face of the Mediterranean guy. The figures left him and moved on to the woman. Two more figures joined them at her side. Sam started to cry and tried not to watch as they went to work on her. Jimmy started to hyperventilate next to him.

What they were doing to the woman was a hundred times worse than the damage they'd inflicted on the Mediterranean guy. She didn't scream or fight them, and that made watching even worse. She just opened her mouth and let out a silent cry of anguish so profound it transcended the desecration of her flesh.

"Aww man, that ain't right!" said someone behind them, his voice loud with disgust. "That ain't right."

Every time Sam or Jimmy tried to close their eyes or turn away Ashkan punched them both in the back of the head. "Ashkan, please man," said Sam. "You don't need to show us anymore. You've made your point; you'll get your money. Honestly, even if I have to sell everything, you'll get your money. Just don't make me watch any more. Please don't make me watch anymore."

The drug in Sam's system made him even more susceptible to the footage. He could feel everything they were doing to the woman. Ashkan ignored his pleas; he was mesmerised and appalled by what was happening on the laptop.

There were groans and cries of disgust from the

other men in the room. "Turn it off man," said one. "Turn it off, we've seen enough." Another man started wailing and broke into a sob.

"Can't turn it off," said Ashkan. "They've got to watch this to the end. They have to learn."

But the men in the room had all had enough. Jimmy heard two of them turn to leave the lock up. "Alright," said Ashkan. "We'll leave them to watch the end of it and we'll go for a smoke."

Ashkan and his men were standing behind Sam and Jimmy. It was more intimidating that way. It also made it hard for Sam to work out what was happening. He glanced away from the screen to look at Jimmy. Jimmy had his eyes tightly shut. He'd had enough, but Ashkan was too distracted to notice.

Sam closed his eyes too. He didn't want to watch any more footage; it was becoming unbearable. The drugs had left his nerve endings raw.

Someone's footsteps approached them. Sam winced automatically, expecting a blow, but the footsteps went straight past him. He heard tapping on the laptop keyboard. Were they trying to switch it off?

"Fuck," a voice said in front of him. Sam didn't recognise it. "Fuck NO! FUCK!"

The sound of something very sharp going into flesh followed. Then a sudden release of breath, as if the air had been knocked out of someone. Cries of alarm and disbelief rang out behind Sam, then broke off, becoming throttled chokes and coughs.

Sam pulled his chin into his chest and hunched his shoulders. Trying to make himself as small as he could while still taped to a chair. He could feel tears welling up behind eyelids that were screwed shut.

EXCERPT FROM *THE FINAL CUT*

The whole lock-up was filled with the wet ripping of torn flesh and the crackling snap of fractured bones. It was like someone had recorded a slaughterhouse and then played it at triple speed. Only the sounds weren't coming from the tinny laptop speaker, they were all around him.

Sam couldn't look, couldn't open his eyes. He just froze. Every sound made him shake more. What were Ashkan and the others doing to Jimmy? Why didn't he scream? How could the noise be so deafening?

Sam was next, he knew that. He gritted his teeth but it didn't hold back the sobs that were breaking from his chest. The front of his jeans became warm and wet as his bladder emptied.

One single thought went round and round in his mind.

Please let it be quick.
Please let it be quick.
Please let it be quick.

Make sure to get a copy of *The Final Cut* to read this whole story in its entirety.

THE END?

Not if you want to dive into more of Crystal Lake Publishing's Tales from the Darkest Depths!

Check out our amazing website and online store
or download our latest catalog here.
https://geni.us/CLPCatalog

Looking for award-winning Dark Fiction?
Download our latest catalog.

Includes our anthologies, novels, novellas, collections,
poetry, non-fiction, and specialty projects.

WHERE STORIES COME ALIVE!

We always have great new projects and content on the
website to dive into, as well as a newsletter, behind the
scenes options, social media platforms, our own dark
fiction shared-world series and our very own webstore.
Our webstore even has categories specifically for KU
books, non-fiction, anthologies, and of course more novels
and novellas.

ABOUT THE AUTHOR

Multiple award-winning author, Jasper Bark is infectious—and there's no known cure. If you're reading this you're already contaminated. The symptoms will manifest any time soon. There's nothing you can do about it. There's no itching or unfortunate rashes, but you'll become obsessed with his mind-bending books.

Then you'll want to tell everyone else about his visionary horror fiction. About its originality, its wild imagination and how it takes you to the edge of your sanity. We're afraid there's no way to avoid this. These words contain a power you're hopeless to resist. You're already in their thrall, you know you are. You're itching to read all of Jasper's bloodstained books. Don't fight this urge, embrace it. You've been bitten by the Bark bug and you love it!

Would you like to read five more of Jasper's books absolutely free?

Of course you would. I mean, who doesn't like free books?

Jasper's infamous novella, *Stuck On You* is now free to own as soon as you join Jasper's cult and sign up to his mailing list through the QR code below.

Don't worry, you won't have to shave your head or unalive any celebrities (for the first couple of years). But you will get all of Jasper's latest, videos, podcasts, blogs, breaking news on upcoming books and other crucial information to help you cyberstalk him.

What's more, you'll get two more short novels, a graphic novel and a spoof picture book, just to sweeten the deal! That's five free books just for signing up. These books are exclusive to this offer. You won't get them anywhere else.

Are we crazy? Of course we're crazy! We're asking you to join Jasper's cult!
And because we know you can't bear to miss out.

Don't be the only weird kid on your block to miss out. Don't delay. Sign up today.

Readers . . .

Thank you for reading *Run to Ground*. We hope you enjoyed this novel. If you have a moment, please review *Run to Ground* at the store where you bought it.

Help other readers by telling them why you enjoyed this book. No need to write an in-depth discussion. Even a single sentence will be greatly appreciated. Reviews go a long way to helping a book sell, and is great for an author's career. It'll also help us to continue publishing quality books.

Thank you again for taking the time to journey with Crystal Lake Publishing.

You will find links to all our social media platforms on our Linktree page.
https://linktr.ee/CrystalLakePublishing

MISSION STATEMENT

Since its founding in August 2012, Crystal Lake Publishing has quickly become one of the world's leading publishers of Dark Fiction and Horror books. In 2023, Crystal Lake Publishing formed a part of Crystal Lake Entertainment, joining several other divisions, including Torrid Waters, Crystal Lake Comics, Crystal Lake Kids, and many more.

While we strive to present only the highest quality fiction and entertainment, we also endeavour to support authors along their writing journey. We offer our time and experience in non-fiction projects, as well as author mentoring and services, at competitive prices.

With several Bram Stoker Award wins and many other wins and nominations (including the HWA's Specialty Press Award), Crystal Lake Publishing puts integrity, honor, and respect at the forefront of our publishing operations.

We strive for each book and outreach program we spearhead to not only entertain and touch or comment on issues that affect our readers, but also to strengthen and support the Dark Fiction field and its authors.

Not only do we find and publish authors we believe are destined for greatness, but we strive to work with men and women who endeavour to be decent human beings who care more for others than themselves, while still being hard working, driven, and passionate artists and storytellers.

Crystal Lake Publishing is and will always be a beacon of what passion and dedication, combined with overwhelming teamwork and respect, can accomplish. We endeavour to know each and every one of our readers, while building personal relationships with our authors, reviewers, bloggers, podcasters, bookstores, and libraries.

We will be as trustworthy, forthright, and transparent as any business can be, while also keeping most of the headaches away from our authors, since it's our job to solve the problems so they can stay in a creative mind. Which of course also means paying our authors.

We do not just publish books, we present to you worlds within your world, doors within your mind, from talented authors who sacrifice so much for a moment of your time.

There are some amazing small presses out there, and through collaboration and open forums we will continue to support other presses in the goal of helping authors and showing the world what quality small presses are capable of accomplishing. No one wins when a small press goes down, so we will always be there to support hardworking, legitimate presses and their authors. We don't see Crystal Lake as the best press out there, but we will always strive to be the best, strive to be the most interactive and grateful, and even blessed press around. No matter what happens over time, we will also take our mission very seriously while appreciating where we are and enjoying the journey.

What do we offer our authors that they can't do for themselves through self-publishing?

We are big supporters of self-publishing (especially hybrid publishing), if done with care, patience, and planning. However, not every author has the time or inclination to do market research, advertise, and set up book launch strategies. Although a lot of authors are successful in doing it all, strong small presses will always be there for the authors who just want to do what they do best: write.

What we offer is experience, industry knowledge, contacts and trust built up over years. And due to our strong brand and trusting fanbase, every Crystal Lake Publishing book comes with weight of respect. In time our fans begin to trust our judgment and will try a new author purely based on our support of said author.

With each launch we strive to fine-tune our approach, learn from our mistakes, and increase our reach. We continue to assure our authors that we're here for them and that we'll carry the weight of the launch and dealing with third parties while they focus on their strengths—be it writing, interviews, blogs, signings, etc.

We also offer several mentoring packages to authors that include knowledge and skills they can use in both traditional and self-publishing endeavours.

We look forward to launching many new careers.

This is what we believe in. What we stand for. This will be our legacy.

Welcome to Crystal Lake Publishing—Tales from the Darkest Depths.

www.ingramcontent.com/pod-product-compliance
Lightning Source LLC
Chambersburg PA
CBHW071834190726
48292CB00005B/1780